SEA CHANGES

a novel

BILL BRANLEY

One Sock Press
Seattle, Washington

SEA CHANGES by Bill Branley

Copyright © 2006 by Bill Branley

Excerpts from *THE OLD WOMEN OF THE OCEAN*, by Pablo Neruda, were translated by Jodey Bateman. Used by permission.

Cover design and interior layout by Ellie Searl, Publishista®

Second Edition, 2014
ISBN: 978-0-9778561-2-1
LCCN: 2014906854

First Edition, 2006
ISBN: 0-9778561-0-0

For more information about this book or the author, please visit www.billbranley.com

One Sock Press
Seattle, Washington

This book is a work of fiction. All characters are the product of the author's imagination. However, many locations described in this novel are real. The author would like to acknowledge and thank the following establishments mentioned in the story:

Blackbird Bakery, Bainbridge Island, WA
Camellia Grill, New Orleans, LA
Kneisel Hall, Blue Hill, ME
Old Town Coffee, Tea and Spice, Alexandria, VA
Pike Place Market, Seattle, WA
The Marriott Hotel, Brooklyn, NY
The Striped Bass, Philadelphia, PA
The Tabard Inn, Washington, D.C.
Town and Country Market, Bainbridge Island, WA
Two Boots Pizza, Brooklyn, NY
Wild Ginger, Seattle, WA
Woo Lae Oak, Arlington, VA

Sea Changes is based on a fiction blog published by the author in 2005. Pictures from the original blog can be viewed at www.billbranley.com.

Edited by Chuck Dervarics and Carole Glickfeld.
Ellie Searl, Publishista®, designed the cover and interior of the second edition.
Jeanette Alexander designed the One Sock Press logo and the cover of the first edition.

ACKNOWLEDGMENTS

THE AUTHOR WOULD LIKE TO thank the following people for their invaluable contributions to this story: Johanna Branley, Mary Mellinger, Aline Songy, Cory Munson, Faith Munson, John Munson, James Branley, Kibby MacKinnon, and all the many readers of *Peggy Finds A Friend* who submitted wonderful and valuable comments.

NOTE FROM THE AUTHOR

WHAT IS IT ABOUT CHANGE that is so hard? We fear it. We imagine the worst. Sometimes, when our present circumstances are not desirable, we decide that a change to the unknown is even more undesirable. We assume the unknown is bad.

In this story are two people you will no doubt recognize. They deal with change in opposite ways: one embraces it and the other is unable to leave the comfort of the familiar.

The story of these particular people is a bit more complicated because each has lost a loved one, and in ways both subtle and not so subtle each is clinging to the past. Opening themselves to change is hard because they must let go of the reassuring sadness of their memories.

When the story opens, Peggy had only recently moved to Bainbridge Island, which is thirty minutes from Seattle by ferry. Her goal was to start a new life a year after her husband's death. She had lived most of her adult life in

Seattle, happily married and raising her children until they were off on their own.

Peggy begins a new daily routine commuting back to Seattle by ferry to her job as an analyst for an environmental nonprofit. She meets Raoul, a fellow commuter, and discovers the challenge of moving on from the past without feeling like she is dishonoring her late husband. Raoul is on a similar journey, but his approach, and his needs, are completely different.

The characters in Sea Changes spend a lot of time talking about current issues, like global warming and homeland security and how communities don't invest enough in infrastructure. Peggy finds these kinds of issues exciting and motivating. She lives for change, and for improvements in the world that help people. But sometimes these same topics can divide people who otherwise care about each other.

Bill Branley
May 2014
Seattle, Washington

ONE

PEGGY HEGGY BOARDED THE MORNING ferry to Seattle just before 5:20 and walked along the corridor to her favorite seat. She preferred the left side of the vessel because it gave her a dramatic view of the city as the ferry made its turn out of the harbor. On this day Seattle was shrouded in mist; the buildings looked dark and ghostly. In her mind there was at least one ghost, that of her late husband, Taylor. She couldn't look anywhere without seeing him.

She hadn't planned to take such an early ferry to work every day. Then again, she hadn't planned to take a ferry at all. It never occurred to her that Taylor would die suddenly at age fifty-nine, leaving her a widow at fifty-seven after thirty years of marriage. Within a span of six hours on a Tuesday evening he went from eating dinner to collapsing from a stroke to being whisked to the emergency room to quietly departing without ever saying good-bye. A year later she gave away many of their possessions, sold the house in

Seattle and rented a small house in a nearby island community, a lively place, with gallery events and shows and concerts going on all the time. She figured she could start a new life there. But she also found that she woke up early, sometimes at four or four-thirty in the morning, and had no desire to linger in the empty bed wishing Taylor were with her.

She was still adjusting to the routine of the ferry. It is a large vessel that can carry two hundred cars and two thousand people on its run between Seattle and Bainbridge Island, where her new house was a short walk from the terminal. She had seen the ferries often from the Seattle side, and had even been on them once or twice. They looked to her like great, floating parking garages. She never imagined that she would be riding one every morning and every afternoon.

Her daughter, Marjorie, had suggested a change. "Why not try living somewhere else, Mom?"

"You mean, like a retirement home?"

"No, of course not. You're too young for that," said Marjorie, who had moved to the East Coast in her mid-twenties and was now married. Her brother, Taylor, Jr., had followed her eastward and settled in Brooklyn, New York. Neither of them was present when their father died.

"I'm glad somebody thinks I'm young," Peggy had said. It was another in their series of what-is-Mom-going-to-do-now discussions.

"You *are* young, and very attractive."

"For heaven's sake, do you want money?"

"Mother!"

In just two weeks of commuting, Peggy discovered that all manner of people ride the ferry: people in pin-striped suits, people in paint-splattered coveralls, people with multicolored hair and facial jewelry protruding from surprising places, and people who aren't distinguishable in any way whatsoever. There are families, sports teams, church groups and school groups. There are old people, young people and all ages in-between.

She noted that some of the morning passengers seemed to simply move their activities from home to ferry without any apparent interruption. They peeled hard-boiled eggs, ate yogurt, prepared cereal and milk, stirred coffee, pored over laptop computer screens or talked on cell phones. Some sat silently daydreaming or dozing, others carried on animated conversations, sometimes non-stop for the entire thirty-five-minute crossing.

As a result of her diligent people-watching, Peggy became intrigued by a man who sat in the next booth down the aisle from her in the mornings and seemed not to know she existed on the same planet. He wore black motorcycle leathers and a neatly trimmed gray beard; his brown reading glasses rested low on his nose as he scanned his newspaper.

She learned his name when, one day, a fellow motorcyclist stopped and addressed him, and they had a brief conversation about brakes or tires, something having to do with motorcycles. Raoul had a pleasant, musical quality to his voice, and friendly eyes. Then one day she became further intrigued when she noticed that beneath his riding outfit he wore a very fine suit and tie. She wondered, at that point, what it might be like to have a male companion who wasn't her husband.

She even learned his full name: Raoul Stein. It was an odd mix of names, she thought. Of course, she had always had an odd mix of names. She was born Peggy Henry and married Taylor Heggy and became Peggy Heggy, which horrified her mother. At the time she didn't see much difference in going from two first names (and not even two girls' names) to two rhyming names. Either way, people paused when they heard it and displayed a certain challenged look in their eyes as they tried to think of an original remark. Besides, being in love with Taylor, she didn't much care what his name was.

Peggy was employed by an environmental nonprofit where, in the course of her duties, she met with government agency officials, big-money donors, famous scientists and, of course, people from other environmental nonprofits. She liked a neat style of dress—crisp and refined, to her, at least—that she felt was appropriate for her work, yet comfortable enough for walking to and from the ferry and around town. On this day she wore black shoes, gray slacks, a cream-colored blouse and a well-fitted jacket that she thought flattered her. She carried a roomy bag over her shoulder that contained her book of the moment—a novel called *The Bear Went Over the Mountain*, by William Kotzwinkle—and a container of tea, a leftover scone that she had made the previous weekend, her lunch, and a bottle of drinking water. She was ready for another day at the office.

As Peggy settled down to read, she peeked over her book and saw Raoul leaning against the window as usual, his attention on the Seattle paper.

Soon she was joined in her booth by Kelly Flinn, a retired music professor whom she had met on her first day riding the ferry. He went to the University of Washington several mornings each week to lead a music workshop.

"Good morning," she said. "How are you?"

"Could be better," said Kelly. "The technology levy failed."

Kelly loved to discuss the issues of the day, even at 5:20 in the morning. This one had to do with a proposal to increase funding for technology in local schools.

"From what I read I think it made sense, but I'm still new to the island," said Peggy.

"People seem to think money grows on trees," said Kelly.

Peggy then noticed, out of the corner of her eye, that Raoul had raised his head from his paper and was looking in their direction.

Kelly continued, "We're constantly asking for the best roads and the best schools and the best services, but nobody wants to pay for them."

Peggy looked at Kelly but strained to monitor Raoul's movements out of her peripheral vision. She wondered if he might join the conversation.

"Mind you, I come from a background in education," said Kelly. "It's more expensive than people think. Nine million is nothing for a school system the size of ours. And do you know what else? Investing in education pays many dividends that you can't always add up on a spreadsheet. Intangibles. People must consider the intangibles." He gestured with long, expressive fingers.

"Do you have family in the school system?" asked Peggy.

"Three grandchildren. And you?"

"I have two grown children living back east. No grandchildren yet." She sighed. Taylor had wanted to be a grandfather.

"Even if you don't have children, the levy would have been a good investment. Good schools draw more families to a community. When you have more families, and this is supported by the data, you see crime going down, and property values going up."

Now Raoul was shifting in his seat. He crossed and re-crossed his legs and rattled his paper. Perhaps he had a difference of opinion with Kelly, she thought. She wanted to know more about him. What did he do? Was he acquainted with Kelly Flinn? Were they political enemies?

The ferry docked on schedule at Pier 52 in downtown Seattle. Peggy said good-bye to Kelly and walked to First Avenue and turned left and walked three blocks to her office building. She rode the elevator to the fifth floor. As she approached the glass doors to her suite, she realized, as she did almost every day, that she didn't need to keep working. The insurance settlement plus their savings left her with enough to live on. But she told herself, as she always did, that she loved her job; she loved the issues, the people, the satisfaction of helping to care for the environment. It was a cause that had been a passion of hers and Taylor's, and she had vowed to continue the work.

In the early afternoon she made the return trip while the sun was still high and the water was very blue. She usually didn't see Raoul or any of her morning commuting companions, which was fine, because in the afternoons she preferred to bury herself in her book rather than converse. When she got home she liked to make tea and sit in a sunny spot in her garden. In those moments she often wondered what Taylor would think of her new lifestyle, and whether he would approve.

Friday, May 20

Peggy boarded the boat, made her way to her favorite seat and was surprised to hear a man's voice say "Good morning." She looked up. Raoul was smiling at her. He had greeted her for the first time!

"Good morning," she said. "I'm Peggy." She was suddenly glad she had worn her long skirt with boots and a pair of seashell earrings that her son had given her as a birthday present.

"I'm Raoul. Very nice to meet you." He made a little wave from his bench in the next booth. As he leaned closer, his motorcycle leathers creaked and she spotted a colorful tie beneath his dark jacket. "I got a chuckle out of you and Kel yesterday," he said. "I was thinking, ol' Kel's got himself a new victim."

Peggy smiled. "Oh, he was all right. Since I'm new I don't mind getting caught up on the local gossip."

"Don't worry, he'll be back to give you another earful. He makes his way 'round to this side of the boat every few days."

Raoul poured a cup of something; coffee, she presumed, from a stainless steel Thermos.

Peggy held up her own Thermos. "We have matching containers. But I suppose yours has coffee."

"Tea," he said, looking up.

"Really? I had labeled you a coffee drinker."

"I enjoy breaking stereotypes," said Raoul.

Peggy laughed. His manner was easygoing.

"So, you just moved to the island. Where from?" he asked.

"Ballard."

"Ah, Ballard. A great old Seattle neighborhood. I lived in Magnolia for many years."

"I love Magnolia. When my late husband and I first went shopping for houses we looked in Magnolia. But then we found the perfect house in Ballard, and at a good price back then."

"Everything was a good price back then," laughed Raoul. "I used to go for walks and I could see Bainbridge

Island, and it looked peaceful and quiet. After about ten years I said to my family, 'Why not move there?'"

She resisted the urge to ask about his family.

Then he said, "I'm sorry to hear about your husband."

She blushed. "I don't usually mention it. I didn't mean to burden you with that."

"It's quite all right. You see, I'm a widower myself."

"Oh," was all Peggy could think of saying. She clammed up, which is exactly what she always did when the topic got around to deceased spouses. She didn't like to discuss Taylor except with her children and a few old friends.

She fumbled with her book. Then he said, "Your book looks interesting."

"It's a very funny story," she said, "about a bear who goes into the city and lives like a human. He wears clothes and rides the subway and eats in restaurants. And people don't seem to notice that he's a bear."

Raoul seemed very amused and it helped Peggy relax. After a while, the conversation lapsed, as it often does on the ferry. People who commute together tend to talk or not talk as the mood suits them. He read his newspaper, she continued her novel.

By 5:40 they were halfway across Puget Sound, and for the first time in many days Peggy saw sunlight on her morning crossing. A shaft of brilliant orange light broke over the Cascades and spilled onto the calm surface of the water. A light mist partially obscured the city, but the overall effect was bright and colorful, with hints of purple and blue and gold in the air. It was a good day to be out, Peggy thought. Today I made a new friend.

Monday, May 23

Peggy hurried from her house to the ferry terminal. She wasn't late, but she was eager to get there. She carried in her shoulder bag a couple of currant scones from a batch she had made the day before. She was nervous about offering one to Raoul. Would he think she was being too friendly? She wondered if she would be breaking some unwritten code of ferry commuters. *Thou shalt not get too personal.*

As she approached her favorite seat she saw with relief that Raoul was in his usual place, dressed in his motorcycle leathers, his white helmet resting next to him on the seat. But then Peggy saw something else: a young woman. She was very pretty, with wavy dark hair and large eyes and creamy skin.

Peggy's first alarming thought was, Oh no, he goes for young girls.

The woman wore her jeans low on the hips the way young girls do now. As Peggy took her seat and stole a few glances at Raoul and his companion, she realized that the young woman must be his daughter. The eyes, cheeks and mouth bore a family resemblance.

Raoul looked up and said, "Good morning."

"Good morning," Peggy said.

"My daughter's visiting from Philadelphia. This is Deidre; Deidre, this is Peggy," said Raoul.

"How do you do?" said Peggy.

"Fine, thank you."

"Are you in town long?" Peggy asked.

Deidre glanced at her father. "Just a few days. It's the anniversary of my mother's death."

Peggy immediately thought of her own children. "I lost my husband just over a year ago." Peggy was talking to

Deidre, but she hoped Raoul was listening. She felt bad for having gone quiet on him the previous day. She wanted him to know the circumstances, at least.

Peggy reached into her bag. "I brought a little snack this morning. I didn't know you would have company, Raoul." She got up and walked around to the booth in which Raoul and Deidre sat. She handed them a scone on a napkin. "Perhaps you two can share."

"Mmm, I'll bet those are delicious," said Deidre, her face lit up.

"That's extremely thoughtful of you," said Raoul. Peggy guessed that it was the first time anyone had brought him scones on the ferry.

Deidre took a bite. "It's really good, Dad. Light, like Mom's."

Raoul sighed. "I'm afraid it's not on my diet, but I will enjoy them vicariously while I watch you spill crumbs on yourself."

"Dad!"

"I had a difficult time making them," said Peggy. "My husband loved these scones."

"I know that feeling," Raoul said. "It's been seven years for us. But I remember so well how it felt the first year. It was like she had just stepped out on an errand. I kept waiting for her to walk through the door. I realized after a while I wasn't living, actually. Just existing, waiting."

"Yes. Yes," said Peggy excitedly. "That's it exactly. That's why I had to move to the island. I had to restart my life. I told people I was moving for the view, but really I just wanted a fresh start." She reached for a tissue and looked down as she dabbed at her eye. There was an awkward silence, which she filled by opening her tea container.

Raoul cleared his throat and said, "Peggy and I have matching Thermos bottles and we both drink tea."

"You didn't tell me you were having so much fun on the ferry, Dad," said Deidre.

Raoul said, "As a matter of fact this is the best day I've had in a long time."

Peggy quickly got out her novel and hid behind the pages.

Tuesday, May 24

Peggy took a later ferry. She had scheduled a routine medical check-up, her first on the island, and the only opening was on a weekday morning.

The sun was high and the water glistened like jewels by the time she boarded the ferry to go to work. As the boat motored out of Eagle Harbor, Peggy noticed the low tide and the birds pecking hungrily at the exposed starfish and shellfish. She also noticed, with interest, a U.S. Coast Guard boat motoring next to them out of the harbor and across the Sound. It was a small orange craft with a tiny cabin and a large machine gun mounted on the front. She could see two sailors in the cabin. Above the cabin was a flashing blue light. She wondered if trouble was expected during the crossing.

Up on deck it was windy and exhilarating. She had to zip up her windbreaker and dig her hands into her pockets. Strands of hair blew around her face. She was just about to go back in when she saw a familiar face.

"Deidre?" Peggy said.

"Oh. Hello, Peggy."

"I take it you didn't ride the 5:20 boat with your father."

"Ugh. I don't know how Dad does that everyday. I did it once to keep him company but that was enough."

"Would you like to get out of this wind?" asked Peggy.

"Sure. There's a shelter over there."

They walked to a covered area containing rows of benches. Peggy kept glancing at the Coast Guard escort, waiting to see if a sailor would run out and fire the machine gun. They sat and had a long view looking south. The green trees and old beachfront hotels of West Seattle soon came into view. Two benches over, a man played guitar.

"What was your husband's name?" asked Deidre.

"Taylor. Taylor Heggy. People thought it was so funny that a girl named Peggy married a guy named Heggy. That's how I became Peggy Heggy. People always said 'Huh?' and I had to explain it."

"It is cute, and unusual, you have to admit," said Deidre.

"What was your mother's name?" Peggy asked.

"Priscilla."

"A lovely name. What was she like?"

"She was a dancer and singer. Very active in local theater. The life of the party you might say."

"I'm sure she is missed."

"She left a gaping hole in the lives of many people."

"Raoul seems to have settled into a new life."

"Don't be fooled. He's still very lonely, I think. In a way I'm glad you and I have had this chance to talk," said Deidre.

"Why's that?"

"You're the first person to draw him out in a long time. He talked about you last night, in an offhand way, pretending like it's nothing. But that's just the macho side of him. There's a very human side of him, too."

"Thank you, Deidre. That's very nice to hear," said Peggy.

Wednesday, May 25

At 5:11 the sky was a cheerful blue and filled with light and color. A few small clouds reflected orange, pink and purple from a sun that glowed brightly from below the horizon.

Instead of going into the cabin, Peggy went straight up on deck to absorb the brilliant morning. Looking over the rail, she saw a full moon hanging low over Eagle Harbor, its nocturnal journey not yet completed. Walking around to the front, she saw the Sound glowing pink and green with sunlight. It was going to be a special day.

"Hello," Peggy said to Raoul, once she made her way to her seat.

"Good morning," said Raoul, leaning back against the window, ignoring the view.

"Can you believe this day?"

"It's a splendid morning," he said, with a quick glance over his shoulder.

"Would you like to go on deck?" She almost regretted saying it, wondering if she was being too bold.

"Well, I suppose a stroll might be nice after we're underway." He seemed very hesitant, so she didn't press the issue.

Then Kelly plopped down next to her.

"Hello, Kel," said Peggy.

His voice was raspy but energetic. "It's going to be another crazy day. This election dispute has become a career move for some people."

She heard Raoul sigh from his bench in the next booth. The disputed Washington State governor's election was a popular topic of conversation.

"The Republicans are still calling it fraud, but nobody's stopping to look at how cumbersome and error-prone the system was to begin with," said Kelly.

As he launched into the arcane details of election laws and procedures, Peggy watched a group of bicycle riders occupy the booth across the aisle. Since the weather was relatively warm, and dry, they wore even less than usual: short biker's tights and thin clingy jerseys. As one woman bent over to unlace her riding shoes, Peggy noted with fascination that her bottom was no wider than a bicycle seat. What do these people eat? she wondered.

"...the system has always been inefficient: lost ballots, incorrectly processed ballots, sloppy work by underpaid workers or well-meaning volunteers who are tired or have poor eyesight," said Kelly with great animation. "What do you expect from that kind of a system? The thing is, if we are serious about having proper elections, then we have to put money into it."

Raoul put down his newspaper and spoke up. "Peggy, did you want to go up on deck? I think we'll have a good view of Rainier."

"What a wonderful suggestion," said Peggy.

Peggy excused herself and accompanied Raoul up the stairs and out onto the windy deck. As they walked she noticed for the first time that he stood a whole head taller than she.

"You looked like a damsel in distress," he said.

"He's really not that bad, you know. He does keep up with the issues." Peggy tugged her wool wrap more tightly around her.

"I suppose I'm just being an old curmudgeon," said Raoul.

Peggy stopped, stunned by the vista. "Look at the view, Raoul. To the east, the Cascade Range, visible from end to end, with Seattle in the foreground looking like a little village. And Mount Baker way up there in the north, and of course, Rainier right there, look how it's glowing orange." She spun around. "And to the west, the Olympic Range, look at those snowy peaks, and look how you can see the whole range. What an incredible morning! You can hardly decide which view to enjoy."

Raoul stood very close to her. "Yes, now that you've pointed it all out to me, it is quite amazing." They stood silently, feeling the moment, then he said, "Peggy, thanks to you, I will never again take these days for granted."

"I love a view by the sea. It changes almost every day, you know," said Peggy. She looked away from him, grinning, and let her shoulder brush lightly against his.

Thursday, May 26

The sky was apricot-colored in the east and blue directly overhead as Peggy walked up the ramp to the ferry. A single long cloud reflected the glow of the sun. The weather report had predicted highs in the 80s. Peggy could feel summer coming on.

Raoul was not wearing his usual motorcycle leathers, just the suit and tie that he normally wore underneath his riding outfit. His beard was neatly trimmed. He was handsome.

"I had to drive the car today," he said, sliding onto the bench next to her. "So I was wondering if you would like to meet for lunch."

"Yes," she said immediately. But inside she was alarmed. A lunch date! She made a quick mental inventory of what she was wearing. It would do—a knee-length skirt with a comfortable top. She hoped it wasn't too casual.

"It's going to be hot today," she said, looking at his suit.

"I work in a law firm; this is the uniform."

He chose a swank lunch spot on Second Avenue, to which he drove them in his black Mercedes. She felt out of place sliding onto the leather seat; the luxury was so foreign to her. Raoul looked dashing at the wheel, with his gray beard and dark suit and smooth, charming voice. She felt she was being pampered. The valet welcomed them and took the car with a note of familiarity; perhaps Raoul was a regular customer there.

Inside, they sat in a cool corner, away from the intense heat of the day, while a demure waitress in a crisp apron brought them sparkling water with lemon. Summer had rushed upon them like a steam engine; everyone was asking where the heat came from. Peggy knew the answer: climate change.

She was familiar with the data on air temperature change through her job, where she was in charge of the Environmental Education Database, a collection of data and references that documented changes in the Earth's climate since the beginning of the Industrial Age.

But she was hardly thinking of that as she sat across a mahogany table from Raoul and fingered the silverware and the cloth napkin. Their conversation was light. Deidre had enjoyed her visit to Bainbridge Island and was back in Philadelphia, where she was earning an M.B.A. at the Wharton School. Raoul asked questions about her children, so she explained that Taylor, Jr., was an aspiring filmmaker in Brooklyn, taking classes at the Pratt Institute and waiting on tables at night. Her daughter, Marjorie, was a statistician who'd married a lobbyist and lived in Arlington, Virginia.

"A statistician married to a lobbyist. Hmm, I would love to hear their dinner conversations," he said with amusement.

"Cryptic is the way I would describe it," said Peggy, enjoying herself.

The trouble started when Raoul talked about his job. She learned he was a lawyer for Burnett and Edwards.

"Burnett and Edwards?" said Peggy almost choking on a piece of ice.

"Have you heard of them?"

"I'll say. My organization frequently opposes them in court."

"Oh? What organization would that be?"

"Northwest Environmental Fund."

He groaned. "I hope you're not one of the militant types."

"I'm not sure how you define the so-called militant types. But we are aggressive about making polluters pay for their crimes."

Raoul shook his head. "Everyone wants everything to be black and white. It's never as simple as that. The firms we represent are following the law."

"That's exactly the problem," said Peggy. "They follow the law, but the laws are too weak. The laws were written by politicians who receive substantial contributions from the nation's leading polluters. Were any of your clients on Dick Cheney's energy task force?"

"I'm not at liberty to say."

"Figures."

His tone softened. "Peggy, you are a very pleasant and attractive woman. Why do you want to bother yourself with politics?"

It was at that moment that Peggy decided she didn't like the sound of his voice. What had earlier seemed musical and charming now sounded condescending and manipulative.

"Because somebody has to not let these energy companies get away with murder. They will rape the environment to make a buck and you know it."

"Look, can't we just have a nice lunch together? Why do you have to bring shop talk into this?"

"Is that what it is to you? Shop talk? One of your clients spilled oil in Puget Sound and tried to keep it a secret. Another of your clients released dangerous chemicals into the Columbia River for years until regulatory action forced them to stop. If it wasn't for the law they would still be doing it."

"There's no proof that those chemicals were harming the environment," said Raoul with a businesslike tone.

The waitress placed a delicious-looking black bean quesadilla in front of Peggy, but she had lost her appetite. In fact she wanted to run from the restaurant. But as she sat there debating whether to do that she blamed herself for agreeing to have lunch with a man she didn't know.

"Raoul, I'm sorry, but this is really difficult for me. I have spent the last twenty years fighting the very organizations that you represent. I can't turn my back on that."

Raoul didn't try to change her mind. They talked about nothing of importance while Peggy nibbled at her food. Afterward, she politely thanked him for the meal and walked back to her office.

She was angry with herself. Why am I chasing after men at my age? I have better things to do, she thought. She decided to forget about Raoul.

TWO

PEGGY GOT UP LATE, THEN dragged herself through her morning routine. When she realized the time, she hurried out the door without taking the lunch she had made. The morning was gray and dark and drizzly. Thick, wet clouds hung low over the water as she approached the terminal.

Raoul was not there, which left her disappointed and then annoyed with herself for being disappointed. Kelly sat next to her and started talking about the gas tax, a new move by the state to raise money for transportation projects. Across the aisle, the bicyclists peeled off wet layers and dried themselves with little towels and chatted about their Memorial Day weekend rides. The highlight for Peggy had been a walk to the Farmer's Market to buy eggs at the 4-H Club booth. They were so fresh that Peggy decided to have fried eggs, over easy, for breakfast, something she could never do with Taylor because of his cholesterol problem.

"I think gas is too cheap in this country," said Kelly.

"It's much more expensive in Europe," said Peggy. She thought about the phone call she had received on Sunday from her daughter.

Marjorie had scolded her for being too harsh with Raoul. "You can't expect everyone to have the same views as you do. Look at you and Dad. How many things did you disagree on?"

The ferry made the turn; Seattle sat across the Sound in swirls of fog and rain and mist. The buildings were dark, but lights twinkled from the highway and the waterfront.

Then Marjorie had said, "You are looking for reasons to not get involved, Mom. You've got yourself convinced that you can't start any new relationships."

"Who's looking for a relationship? Isn't thirty years with one man enough?" Peggy had said.

Peggy turned to Kelly, determined to get him onto a non-political subject. "What kind of music do you teach at U.W.?"

Kelly seemed to be taken by surprise, but quickly switched gears. "Jazz," he said. "You see, I have this improvisation workshop called C changes."

"As in the letter 'C'?"

"Yes. It's about chord progressions in the key of C, but you can apply it to all keys. The point is the way in which you depart from the home key in your composition. You transition to other keys, and then you return."

"Very interesting," she said. "It's all about transition and change."

"Constant change. In music you never sit still," Kelly said.

"I'm afraid my musical knowledge is fairly limited. I enjoy chamber music, especially Baroque."

"Ah, some of the Baroque masters wrote more jazz than jazz composers today," said Kelly.

She smiled. "Kelly, this has been a great chat."

As the ferry glided into its slip at the Seattle terminal, Peggy walked forward and stood on deck in the gray mist with her fellow passengers, most of whom silently watched the ferry attendant. Peggy recalled the phrase "huddled masses" and it made her feel like an immigrant arriving by boat. But I've lived in Seattle for thirty years, she thought. Today she was especially struck by the newness of her surroundings and her lifestyle; she was an immigrant of sorts. She had spent most of her adult life in Ballard, raising her children and being married to Taylor. Now, in just a few short weeks, she had taken up a new life, living on the island with new people and riding the ferry to work. But she wasn't sure how new she really wanted her life to be. Did she want to forget the past? That was impossible. But it boiled down to this, as she saw it: Should she let herself become a different kind of person, perhaps a person that Taylor would not have wanted to marry? Should she still be Taylor's wife?

While she waited, she leaned over the rail to look at the car deck. The bicycle riders were waved off, followed by the motorcyclists. Peggy spotted Raoul on a fat blue bike. He looked dashing and confident. She wondered where he had sat during the crossing. Apparently, he had avoided her.

Wednesday, June 1

Peggy hurried to the terminal in high spirits. Not even the gray rolling clouds overhead could dampen her mood. It was one of those dark yet dramatic mornings, where clouds stretch to the horizon in different shades of gray and green and black. The calm waters of the Sound glowed with a soft greenish light that broke through openings in the cloud cover. It was through one of those openings that Peggy could see a wisp of a crescent moon hanging in the sky. It seemed to smile down on her; today would be a good day.

In her backpack she carried two bran muffins, each stuffed with raisins and bits of dried apricot. She had kept up a running conversation with her daughter while making the muffins the night before.

"Of course you're doing the right thing," Marjorie had said.

"I don't know. It all seems so silly," complained Peggy, although secretly she was enjoying herself. She had made up her mind to approach Raoul with a peace offering. The more she thought of it, the more embarrassed she became over her behavior at the restaurant. In reflection, it seemed so childish.

"It's not silly," Marjorie said. "Look, pretend you're forming a club and you want to recruit him as a member. Call it the Sixtyish Singles' Club."

"I am not sixty," Peggy said.

"Sorry, but the fifty-eightish singles' club doesn't sound as good," said Marjorie over the phone.

"Oh, whatever. I'm making low-fat bran muffins; he's watching his weight, you know."

"That's the spirit. Gotta run. 'Bye."

Then Taylor, Jr., called. He was less supportive. "How can you make bran muffins for a lawyer who defends the nation's worst polluters? I thought you had values, Mom."

"I do have values." Her son was going to be one of those strident documentary filmmakers. Everything was black and white to him, no pun intended. "It's just that, well, you need to hear people out. Besides, there are many famous cases of couples who come from opposite ends of the political spectrum."

"Are you thinking of marrying this guy?"

"No, of course not. I'm just using an example to make my point." Her son had as much appreciation for nuance as a Labrador.

Now as she walked briskly to her usual seat, she was thinking of how good it was going to feel to make peace with Raoul, to unburden herself.

She rounded a corner and entered the aisle. She looked ahead. Raoul was in his customary spot. A woman sat with him, and this was definitely no daughter visiting from out of town. She was in her late forties, very well dressed in a pin-striped business outfit with a silky blouse. Her hair was a shade of blonde that Peggy could not even name and she wore lots of makeup. She was attractive in a way that appealed to many men.

Peggy's heart sank and her steps slowed as she approached. She took her seat quietly, not wanting to attract attention.

"Good morning," Raoul said, smiling.

"Good morning, Raoul," said Peggy. "It's very good to see you again."

"It's good to see you. This is Florence. She's an old friend who has just moved to Bainbridge Island."

"Welcome to the neighborhood," said Peggy, "although I'm brand new myself." The woman's skirt seemed short for a professional type.

Peggy poured herself some tea and left the bran muffins in her backpack. She figured her officemates would appreciate them.

Friday, June 3

She overslept. It didn't surprise her. Peggy had discovered that by the end of the week she was so tired from waking up early that she was destined to oversleep sooner or later. She was angry with herself at first, then decided it was a good excuse to take the day off. Her boss, Milton, was generally very understanding.

Faced with a long day and no firm plans, she rummaged through a collection of brochures and found one that described scenic walks on Bainbridge Island. Since she had not yet ventured to the west side of the island, she decided to try the walk along Crystal Springs Drive, near the water.

By late morning Peggy was in her car, driving to the small community of Lynwood on the other side of the island. She wore walking shoes and shorts and a hat; on the seat beside her was a small backpack with a Thermos of tea and her sunglasses. Peggy parked near the small coffee shop at Lynwood Center, planning to get something to take on her walk. A black Mercedes in the spot next to her seemed familiar. Inside the shop, she was dazzled by the mouth-watering display of baked goods and hardly paid attention to the other customers.

A man behind her said, "I recommend the marble pound cake." She turned. It was Raoul. He was dressed in shorts and hiking boots and wore a hat.

"What a surprise!" said Peggy.

"I thought it would be a nice day for a walk," he said. "I took the day off."

She laughed. "I took the day off because I overslept."

"Where are you walking?" he said.

"I was going to walk along Crystal Springs Drive. Is it nice?"

"It's perfect. Would you like some company?"

She felt herself blush. "Why, uh, sure."

Peggy bought a piece of cake, and Raoul purchased a bottle of water. Five minutes later they were out in a gray, overcast day, walking along a marsh that bordered the road, breathing in salty air and the aroma of cedar and fragrant flowers.

"Thank goodness the cottonwood trees have finished shedding," said Raoul.

"Oh, that was something," she said. "It looked like snow, the air was so thick with floating bits of cotton."

They chatted casually as they walked along, talking about their homes and life on the island, and what their children were doing. Peggy realized that they were sticking to safe topics. She wondered how long it would be until they ran out of things to talk about.

Finally, Raoul blurted out, "Do you know I was happily married for twenty years to a woman who didn't agree with me on anything? We went to different churches because I wouldn't change my religion and she wouldn't change hers. I voted Republican, she voted Democrat. She donated time and money to arts organizations, I played golf. She had friends who were male, female, black, white, gay, straight. My friends were rich, white males. The point is, How did we get along? How did we ever fall in love to begin with? To tell you the truth, I don't really know. It just happened. When the chemistry is right, all the other things don't matter."

With each word of Raoul's speech, Peggy felt herself grow lighter and lighter. By the time he finished talking, she was weightless. She stopped and took his hand. "Raoul, you are a lot wiser than I've given you credit for. I'm sorry for thinking poorly of you."

He kissed her hand; she felt a tingle run up her arm. "Thank you for listening," he said. "It means a lot to me."

They continued their walk, still holding hands, and Peggy suddenly had the feeling that they could talk about anything.

Wednesday, June 8

It was only a matter of time, Peggy knew, before she would ask Raoul for a ride on his motorcycle. She was attracted to the idea of it, but frightened at the same time. After much badgering on her part, Raoul finally agreed.

He arrived with a roar at her doorstep in the late afternoon after work. Peggy briefly wondered what her neighbors would think of this dashing man on a motorcycle coming to pick her up. As promised, he brought a helmet, a yellow one, which closed around her head like a glove and made her feel as if she were going on a space journey. She wore jeans and hiking boots, with the laces tucked in, plus a corduroy shirt with a scarf and an old denim jacket that she had not worn in ten years. The bike seemed fat and low as she swung her leg over it and settled onto a small seat immediately behind Raoul. She noticed there was nothing to hold on to, so she figured she would hold on to him.

When Raoul started the machine, she felt the vibrations roll from her legs to her head. Her hands rested on her knees, but as soon as he turned the bike and accelerated out of the driveway, she threw her arms around his waist without hesitation. She was awed by the sensations of speed and power, and the surprising smoothness of the ride. When he reached Fletcher Bay Road, she tightened her grip on him and drew closer as her body leaned with his into the turns, swooping beneath tall, dark evergreens that bordered the road.

The sky darkened quickly as they neared Battle Point Park after a rollercoaster ride on a narrow, hilly road, leaving Peggy clinging to Raoul for dear life. Their timing was fortunate. The sky opened up, dumping a wall of rain on them just as they were dismounting near a picnic shelter. Peggy ran across a patch of wet grass, her vision partially obscured by the helmet. She didn't see the slight depression in the ground. Her foot turned as it landed in the low spot, and she fell forward onto a sheet of water and came down hard on her right arm. Raoul was immediately behind her. She felt him lift her quickly and carry her out of the rain.

The pain in her arm was intense; she knew something was wrong with it. Raoul pulled off her helmet.

"Are you okay?"

"I'm not sure." Her right side was soaked. Raoul ran back to the bike and returned with a plastic bag in which he kept a towel. She tried to remove her wet denim jacket but winced uncomfortably.

"Let me help you." Raoul very gently removed the jacket and rolled up the right sleeve of her shirt. "I'm going to touch the arm."

He did, and she said "Ouch."

With her good arm, she started to pat herself dry with the towel. The rain roared around them. Then she laughed. "This is absolutely crazy. I'm fifty-eight years old. I should be home knitting."

He took the towel and pressed it against her back and right side. "I'm sorry you got hurt, but I'm very glad that you aren't home knitting."

The downpour stopped as quickly as it had started, leaving the green surroundings of the park dripping and steaming. Raoul offered to call for an ambulance on his cell phone.

"Oh no," said Peggy. "I really think I can ride back. I can hold on with my good arm and I'll be fine if you go slow."

Raoul looked extremely concerned. "Okay, but we're going straight to the clinic to have it looked at."

Forty minutes and an X-ray later, she came out of an examining room wearing a sling and found Raoul waiting for her.

"A sprain," she said, smiling.

"Thank goodness it wasn't worse." He had a genuine look of relief in his face.

Without a second thought, they hugged each other for several long seconds. Peggy felt a certain amount of stress drain away from her body. She was aware of no pain and completely forgot that her clothes were still as damp as a dishcloth. "I know you won't believe this, but I had a wonderful time," she said.

"I feel terrible."

"Don't. I can't wait to do it again. But on a dry day."

Raoul walked her home, since her house was close to the clinic. She had to assure him over and over that she would be all right. Finally, they said good night and he left.

Later, Peggy realized that she had gone many hours without thinking of Taylor. She had done something completely new and different from anything she and Taylor had ever done together. Regardless of what became of her relationship with Raoul, he had helped her take a small step towards independence.

THREE

Friday, June 10

"THIS IS MY LAST DAY of commuting on Friday," Peggy said to Raoul. "I'm simply too tired by the end of the week."

"Going to a four-day work week?" asked Raoul.

"In theory it'll be a four-day week, but I'm sure I'll end up doing work at home on Fridays. My office is so busy right now."

Raoul grinned. "Whenever the environmentalists get busy, the lawyers get busy, too."

Peggy laughed. "I'll see you in court." Then she thought, happily, at least they could laugh about their differences.

They looked out at a fine mist that settled over Puget Sound. It was one of those days that could be hazy or clear or cloudy. "Even after years of doing this, the early wake-ups tend to make me sleepy by the end of the week," he said.

"Have you thought of retiring early?"

"Oh sure. I'd love to, but I'm committed to seeing a few projects through. Then I plan to play music and tend my garden."

"Tell me about your garden," Peggy said. "I imagine it to be well established, with mature rhododendrons and tall, flowering clematis."

"Right on both counts. Lots of things are in bloom at the moment: lavender, bellflower, peonies…" He stopped.

"Yes?"

"It just occurred to me that perhaps you'd enjoy seeing my garden. It's really quite nice."

"I would love to. I need some social contact on the island."

"In that case I will invite over a few neighbors. I could probably get Ted to bring his lute. I can get out my recorder and we'll attempt to entertain you."

Peggy was thrilled, and a little bit nervous. She was actually going to his house. It would be more than a casual visit, no matter how much she tried to pretend otherwise. She liked Raoul, and it worried her.

"I'm free all weekend," she said.

"Let's try for Saturday afternoon," he said.

She smiled warmly. "Thanks. I can't wait."

But later in the day Raoul called Peggy with disappointment in his voice. "I'm afraid I need to call off our little garden visit this weekend."

"What happened?"

"I'm going to Westport."

"Westport?" Peggy was familiar with Westport, an old fishing town on the Pacific coast, in the southwest corner of Washington.

"You see, my sister has a house there, and in June she normally goes with a group of people; they've been meeting there for forty years. Well, my sister's husband passed away last year, but she still wants to do it, and now she needs my help getting the house ready for her visitors."

"I understand," said Peggy. "I think you should go and help her."

There was a pause. "How would you like to go with me?"

The thought terrified her. "Me? I couldn't possibly on such short, uh, well, there's so much to..."

"It's a big house. You would have your own room, of course," he said.

Peggy was touched by the tone of his voice. He wanted her to be comfortable. "As a matter of fact, I think I can rearrange my schedule," she said. Actually, she had no schedule to rearrange.

By seven o'clock on a bright evening they were headed west in Raoul's car, with Raoul making lots of small talk and Peggy filled with anxiety about the weekend.

"Look at the foxglove," he said, pointing to a hillside covered with tall purple-and-white blossoms. "Would you mind if I get a picture?"

"I don't mind a bit," Peggy said.

Raoul pulled over and walked a few feet off the road, camera in hand. He leaned over a small gulley to get just the picture he wanted, but then his foot slipped into a patch of muddy water. He came back muttering to himself as he threw his muddy shoes into the trunk. Peggy couldn't help giggling as they pulled away.

"I hope it's a good picture," she said.

"Better be."

It was late when they arrived at a beach house about midway between Westport and Grayland. The sound of the ocean triggered a flood of memories in Peggy's mind. She stepped out of the car and walked a few yards to the top of a nearby dune. The very last bit of daylight disappeared beyond the horizon while layers of white foamy surf crashed against the sand, a scene that she and Taylor had witnessed many times on their numerous trips to the shore. They had even spent a few weekends not far from where she stood; they loved it because it was quiet and relatively undeveloped.

Raoul's sister, Francine, was in her late sixties and very jolly. She greeted Peggy in a motherly way that made Peggy feel as if she was Raoul's girlfriend from college, coming to meet the family for the first time. Francine, or Fran, as she liked to be called, showed Raoul to his room and Peggy to hers, and then said, "Don't worry, I'll be in the middle, standing guard." Raoul rolled his eyes and Peggy turned red.

Around the house were pictures of Fran's husband, standing next to his catch of giant halibut or Chinook salmon on the Westport dock. Several trophy fish were mounted on the walls of the living room. Almost every corner was jammed with fishing and clamming paraphernalia, boots, poles, shovels and baskets. It reminded Peggy of her trips to the shore with Taylor and the children.

"We used to dig for razor clams near here," said Peggy, settling down with a glass of beer. Raoul sat next to her on the sofa.

"Oh yes, that was the thing to do," said Fran. "Did you know that a hundred years ago people camped out on the beach for the entire summer? They caught razors by the wagon-load and hauled them down the shore to a cannery that operated twenty-four hours a day."

"Amazing," said Peggy. "I'll bet it didn't take long to completely eliminate the clam population at that rate."

"I think the legal limit now is fifteen clams per person," said Raoul. "It's absurd."

"The alternative is no clams at all," said Peggy firmly. It occurred to her that this weekend would be a good opportunity to teach Raoul something about the environment.

Saturday, June 11

The morning arrived gray and windy and wet. Peggy gingerly pulled on a light jacket—her sprain still bothered her—and took her mug of tea alone out to the beach. She followed the trail to the top of the dune and was surrounded by green and brown beach grasses, tossing and waving, reflecting the gray light to create a shimmering effect. The beach itself was very wide and flat and empty. Peggy thought it must have been a quarter of a mile from the dune to the water's edge as she walked across the hard-packed sand. The roaring surf and mist stretched as far as she could see. It felt as if she were shipwrecked on a deserted island.

In the house, Peggy made toast and helped Francine get her kitchen ready for visitors. The refrigerator needed a good cleaning, and some of the serving platters and cookware had gotten dusty since the last visit. Meanwhile, Raoul fixed a toilet and got firewood.

"I imagine you have many memories here," said Peggy.

"Too many," said Fran. "We used to come out at least five, six times a year. Sid was so crazy about fishing."

"Is this your first visit since your husband died?" asked Peggy.

"Yes, but I promise I won't get too morbid about it."

"Don't worry. I'm going through the same thing. I can picture what it's like for you, being here, with all these things, all these reminders."

"Our wedding china is here," said Fran. "We used it for fish fries on the deck." She laughed. "Sid was never much for being formal about meals."

"I wish I could have met him."

"Raoul tells me your loss is fairly recent."

"Last April," said Peggy. "I'm afraid I don't have as good an attitude as you do. I'm still struggling."

"It's all an act, Sweetie. I can barely get through some days."

"Thanks. I'm glad to hear I'm not alone."

Later in the morning Raoul, Peggy and Fran went to the Westport waterfront to shop for fish. They were surprised to find a pirate-themed street festival in progress, in spite of a light rain. The main street along the waterfront was lined with vendors offering funnel cakes, colorful scarves and skirts, wood carvings, pirate hats, squishy parrot dolls, hand-painted saw blades, trinkets made of bits of twisted metal, and many long strands of colorful beads.

A rock band was tuning up for a concert. Many visitors wore pirate costumes, and Peggy kept bumping into people with three-cornered hats, arm hooks, lots of beads, skulls and crossbones, eye patches and high black boots. Raoul was constantly snapping away with his camera.

Fran pointed. "This looks interesting."

A replica of a pirate ship on wheels had been parked in an empty lot, and in front of it a man dressed as a pirate talked to a gathering crowd. Around him, perched on various pieces of driftwood, were several varieties of parrots.

"All birds are divided into groups called orders." The pirate held a large macaw upside down and pointing to its claws. "There are twenty-seven orders of birds on Earth. Parrots have their own order because they have a feature that makes them distinct from other birds. Does anyone know what that feature is?"

After a few wrong guesses by members of the audience, the pirate explained, "Look at the toes: two toes in the front and two in the back. That's unique in the bird kingdom. It allows them to grip things very well, and helps give parrots their amazing sense of balance."

He twirled the macaw right side up and stroked its chin. Then he went to an African gray parrot and said, "What's your favorite bird?"

The parrot answered in a clear voice, "Purple bird." The pirate translated, "He means hyacinth macaw."

When they were driving back to the beach house, Raoul said, "You know, I actually learned a lot from that guy. For example, I didn't know that parrots can live to be over a hundred years old."

Fran chuckled. "You never know what you might learn at the Westport pirate festival."

In the late afternoon, Raoul and Peggy walked on the beach and took more pictures. Although the sun came out, the wind also picked up. Peggy felt a chill go through her; Raoul gave her his jacket.

After a lengthy walk, they returned to the beach house. Raoul started a fire in the brick-lined pit behind the house, and when it was reduced to smoldering coals he laid pieces of marinated halibut and salmon on a rack and placed it over the heat. Peggy, Raoul and Fran sipped white wine and sat in folding chairs near the fire. When the fish was almost done, Raoul laid down strips of zucchini over the heat and turned them frequently until they were roasted. They ate outside on trays, using Fran's wedding china.

"Just like old times," Fran said.

Peggy detected a note of sadness in her voice. At the same time, she herself felt happier than she had been in a long time. Raoul and Fran were fun to talk to and relaxing to be with.

Peggy took Raoul's hand and kissed it. He raised his glass in a little toast.

Fran cleared her throat. "I'm going to have to keep my eye on you two."

Peggy blushed for the second time in two days.

Then the rain began to fall. Peggy and Fran rushed the trays inside while Raoul gathered up the chairs and took the cooking racks from the fire pit. Afterwards they sat in the living room and drank wine as the rain beat hard against the large plate glass windows. Peggy could see the glass vibrating. She went to the window and saw the dune grasses flattened by the strong winds.

"It'll blow over," said Raoul.

Rainstorms in the Northwest often do end as quickly as they begin, especially in summer, but this one persisted. The three of them sat together quietly, listening to the wind.

"I'm so glad you're here," said Fran. "I would hate to be alone on a night like this."

Raoul yawned. "You can turn some music on if you need a distraction."

"Good idea," said Peggy. She browsed through the many recordings that stood in a neat row on a shelf and settled on Frank Sinatra. It occurred to Peggy that "Stella by Starlight" sounded unusually melancholy against a backdrop of driving rain and howling wind.

They soon went to bed, and Peggy fell asleep quickly. It seemed like only moments had passed, however, when she woke up suddenly and sat upright. She felt something wet on her face. Above her a window had been pushed open by the wind; it was the kind of window that swung inward on hinges. She was disoriented at first, trying to remember where she was, but eventually she recalled Raoul and Fran and coming to Westport, and the storm that must have blown the window open.

She got up to close the window, but when she placed her foot on the floor she felt cold water. *Slosh*. She gasped. The room was flooded. Peggy knelt on the bed to close the window. Then she leaned over to grope for the floor with her hands in the darkness. About an inch or two of water. It felt sandy. She touched her fingers to her mouth. Saltwater. What had become of Raoul and Fran?

Peggy removed her socks and tiptoed across the flooded floor to the hallway. It, too, was filled with water. She went to Fran's room and opened the door. Fran was still sleeping. Peggy went to Raoul's room and shook him. It felt strange to touch him while he was sleeping. What would he think? She wished she had brought a robe.

"What is it?" He sat up quickly.

"The house is flooded."

"What?" He jumped out of bed. Peggy heard him splashing across the room and could barely see his outline in the gloom. She heard his voice. "Would you mind waking up Fran while I try to figure out what's going on?"

Fran sat up and cried when Peggy explained what had happened. She heard Raoul's voice from the hallway. "It's worse than I thought. Come see this."

Peggy held Fran around the shoulders and led her down the hallway, feeling her way with one hand on the wall. Fran muttered something about her carpet being ruined. In the living room, where they had sat and drank wine and listened to Frank Sinatra a few hours earlier, the three of them stopped and stared. Fran cried hysterically. They could see, through the window, a glint of light on water, a large body of water. The Pacific Ocean had broken over the dune and surrounded the house. They were standing in sea water.

Even though Fran's house was built off the ground, enough water had spilled over to reach up to the lower part of the house and cover the floors. Peggy went to the front window to make sure she wasn't imagining things. The storm had passed, leaving a partially cleared sky with a few twinkling stars. There was no beach and no dune, just water. It was as if they were adrift at sea.

Raoul went to the back window and said, "Both cars are submerged."

"What should we do?" asked Fran, tears streaming down her cheeks. "There's no power and no heat."

Raoul turned on a portable radio. They immediately heard news of widespread flooding up and down the coast. A couple of shelters had been set up at churches and community centers.

"We have the canoe. We could paddle to high ground and then try to catch a ride to a shelter."

"Do you have an attic?" asked Peggy.

"We do," said Raoul. "It's dry, but there's no heat."

"Do you have sleeping bags?"

Fran wiped her tears. "Yes. Thank goodness Sid always kept them up on a shelf, in this closet right here." She opened a door. "They're dry," she said proudly. "And we have extra blankets."

Raoul said, "Are you thinking we should try to stay here until daylight?"

"I think it would be safer," said Peggy. "You don't know what's in these waters. And what if we get lost? All of the usual landmarks are under water."

"Good point," he said.

They climbed a ladder to the attic and Raoul spread out the bags and blankets while Peggy stood and shivered. She helped Fran get into her sleeping bag, then Peggy slid in next to Raoul.

"I hope you don't mind," she said, "I need warmth."

"Mind? We should get flooded more often."

The three of them hardly slept. Between the hard floor and the cold and thoughts of rising ocean water beneath them, they couldn't do much more than stare at the rafters that held up the roof. Peggy listened to the creaking and groaning of the house as it shifted, and she pictured it floating out to sea.

When it was light, they heard voices calling out. Raoul ran down the ladder and leaned out of a window and talked to someone who had come by boat to check on them. Within a few minutes they had gathered up some clothing and a few essentials and were in a rowboat heading to dry land. Fran could not stop sobbing at the sight of her flooded house as they rowed away.

Most of Sunday was spent traveling back to Seattle by bus. There was little to be done with the beach house until the flood waters receded. Raoul called to notify Fran's insurance company, and then called his own to report his ruined car. The day was clear and sunny, but they sat glumly in their seats during the journey. From the bus station in Seattle they took a taxi to Fran's house. Raoul borrowed Sid's old car and drove himself and Peggy back to Bainbridge Island on the ferry.

They collapsed into a seat, tired and groggy. Peggy leaned against Raoul and closed her eyes. He put his arm around her. She felt bad for Fran and her beach house full of memories, and she tried to focus on ways in which she could help. Mostly her thoughts were on Raoul and the realization that it would be okay to start a new relationship with someone. She was not afraid of liking him.

FOUR

Monday, June 13

WHEN PEGGY ARRIVED AT WORK the morning after her Westport weekend, her boss, Milton Pacer, called her into his office.

"Did you hear about the coastal flooding?" he asked.

"Did I hear about it? I was in it!" She told him her story of the weekend at Fran's house.

"Wow!" he said. "That's perfect. In fact, your personal account will help add some color to our story. The board held an emergency meeting by phone last night to discuss our response to the flooding. It sounds like we're going to join a lawsuit against the state."

Peggy was not surprised. The Northwest Environmental Fund frequently took on government agencies and corporations in high-profile environmental cases. "Let me guess, they shouldn't have allowed development on that land in the first place."

"Bingo," said Milton. "They caved in to big business and did a disservice to the taxpayers of Washington."

Peggy was intrigued. "So what's my role?"

"It's what you do best: Get our project database organized. You have a lot of it already. There's data on water levels, precipitation, beach erosion, and human activities going back a hundred years. Plus, we have policy experts going over all of the legislation and government studies."

"Sounds exciting," Peggy said. She spent the rest of the day working on her new project. By Monday evening there were news reports from Olympia, the state capital, that opposing sides were lining up over the flooding. Finger pointing was rampant.

Tuesday, June 15

Raoul said, "You won't believe what happened."

"What?"

"The legal aftermath of that weekend flood is almost as bad as the flood itself. Everybody's filing lawsuits: property owners, insurance companies, you name it."

"Don't forget environmental groups."

He looked at her, "Are you saying that your group is jumping on this bandwagon?"

"I wish you wouldn't call it a bandwagon. There are some serious issues at stake."

"I'll say," said Raoul. "That's why the state has hired us to represent them."

Peggy looked at him with surprise. "In that case we shouldn't discuss the matter. Because N.E.F. is joining a lawsuit against the state."

"For what? They're the good guys in all of this."

"There are certain state agencies that are too cozy with property owners. They consistently take the property rights view at the expense of the environment."

"That's why we pay them good tax dollars, to make sure our hard-earned property rights are protected."

"At what cost? Does that mean any old Tom, Dick or Harry can put up a building on a fragile piece of land just because he happens to own it?"

Raoul sighed and rolled his eyes. "Peggy, these issues are very complex."

"Too complex for our little minds to understand? Is that what you mean? You know, you property rights people are always hiding behind this argument that everything's so complex and abstract. But it's really simple. When property owners discover they can make money off their land, they don't want anybody standing in their way. And the state just lets them do what they want because there are tax revenues involved."

"That's absurd. You can't make a charge like that stick."

"We'll see, won't we?"

Wednesday, June 16

Raoul came armed with newspaper clippings.

"You can clearly see how the state has followed the law in permitting coastal development over several decades."

"Of course," said Peggy. "It's easy when you conveniently write laws in such a way that the hard issues are pushed to the sidelines. Any scientist who has studied that coastal region can tell you it should not have been developed."

Raoul tapped his fingers on his leg impatiently. "There you go again, treating these tough issues like they're black and white. This is no business for amateurs."

She looked at him sternly. "I'm not comfortable with that remark. The N.E.F. hires very good people. Let me explain something about that coastline. You know the sand dune that was in front of your sister's house? The one we walked over?"

"Sure. It's been there for decades."

"It's not supposed to be there," said Peggy. "It's only there because a hundred years ago the cranberry farmers along the coast planted non-native beach grasses to stop sand from blowing into their cranberry bogs. Those grasses spread like crazy. They're beautiful to look at today, but the result has been an artificial sand dune that could be covered over with ocean water at any time. Your sister and her husband got lucky all these years. But Nature caught up with them."

"Try telling her that," snapped Raoul.

"I'm sorry about Fran's property. But my belief is that the state should never have permitted construction there in the first place."

"The property was owned fair and square, and the development was perfectly legal," said Raoul.

"Therein lies the rub. It always comes back to property owners and letting them do what they please in the name of tax revenue."

"That's a tough one to prove in court."

"Like I said, we have very good people," she replied.

Thursday, June 16

Upon arriving at her office, Peggy learned from Milton that the governor had convened a Coastal Planning Task Force to study coastal development and its impact on the environment, especially with regard to flooding.

"Great," Peggy said.

"Glad you think so," he said. "We've been invited to participate, and I'm assigning you and Dr. Forest to the task force. There's going to be a meeting at the Seattle Public Library with a teleconference hookup to Olympia. I need you and him to be there."

Close to two o'clock that afternoon, Peggy and Dr. Forest, a marine biologist, walked to the library.

"It's astonishing that we've been invited to attend," said Dr. Forest. "We're usually the ones they keep out of these things."

"That's because they don't like facts getting in the way of their conclusions," Peggy said.

The conference room at the library was crowded. Dr. Forest was greeted by several colleagues who pulled him away. Peggy sat in one of the few empty seats along a wall to the right. Out of the corner of her eye she saw a man take the seat next to her. She turned. It was Raoul.

"What are you doing here?" Raoul asked.

"My organization has been invited to the task force. Somebody has to keep things honest."

Raoul groaned. "This is going to be a three-ring circus."

A woman brought the meeting to order, and then a large screen beamed the governor's image from Olympia. The governor talked for several minutes about the mission of the Coastal Planning Task Force.

"She's really good, isn't she?" whispered Peggy to Raoul.

"She stole the election," said Raoul.

"She won the recount fair and square," said Peggy.

After the presentation, the woman who had brought the meeting to order announced that attendees would be assigned to small committees. Each committee would nominate topics to be formally studied by the task force.

"We're deliberately mixing people up," said the organizer. "The governor wants interaction between government agencies, the private sector, special interests, and academia. All relevant topics are on the table."

When the list was published, Peggy and Raoul discovered that they were assigned to the same committee.

"What fun! We'll work together," said Peggy.

"If this committee does anything resembling work I'll be amazed," he said.

Peggy quickly scanned a fact sheet describing their mission. "We get to look at property rights versus conservation. That's perfect."

"I already know what my recommendation's going to be," said Raoul as they were leaving the library. "Our whole society is based on private ownership of property and the rights that come with it."

"But with rights come responsibilities," said Peggy.

Monday, June 20

Peggy sipped her tea and ran her eye over a list of points Raoul had prepared for discussion.

"Raoul, you aren't taking this seriously, are you? Your proposals are so obviously one-sided. It's as though you're simply dismissing this whole effort as not worth your time."

"These task forces are designed to do one thing: win points with the public. Nothing of consequence ever comes out of them," said Raoul.

"That's such a negative outlook," said Peggy. "If that's the way you feel, why bother?"

"Because I have a boss who wants me to do it and so I am."

"I also have a boss who wants me to do it, and I'm going to see to it that our work has an impact."

"Good luck."

"I'm not letting you off that easy. I want you to put some real thought into this. Don't just treat it like a paper drill."

"If any of this ever sees the light of day it will be amazing."

"What about those birds you took pictures of the other day? The killdeer. Are you willing to say that anyone who owns beachfront property can just bulldoze away the bird habitat and build a big ugly boathouse for their noisy motorboats?"

"Depends. Will they invite me to go water skiing?" chuckled Raoul.

Peggy looked away in frustration. She wanted to scream.

Raoul placed a hand on her arm. "Okay. I'll take it seriously. Our voices will be heard."

She handed him his list of ideas and a pen. "Good. Start revising."

He took the pen. "Me and my big mouth."

Wednesday, June 22

It was a gray morning, misty, cloudy, not a trace of the friendly orange-and-pink glow that Peggy had come to enjoy on her walks to the 5:20 ferry. Yesterday had been the summer solstice, the longest day of the year. She had gone to Raoul's house, finally, to see his garden and hear his renaissance ensemble, which consisted of Raoul on alto recorder, his friend Ted on lute, a white-haired woman named Xena on viola da gamba, and Xena's granddaughter, Laura, on bass recorder. Many of Raoul's flowers were in bloom and he took great delight in discussing each one.

The evening was a success; the band played wonderful music and Xena sang bawdy medieval tunes. Peggy stayed up too late, had too much wine, and was now groggy as she boarded the ferry and found her way to her seat.

Kelly was holding forth on the topic of the day. "I don't know how they expect this coastal task force to get anything done," he said.

"My thoughts exactly," said Raoul. "Committees are by nature inefficient."

"Raoul, a dialogue is needed," said Peggy, pouring tea from her Thermos. "How else can people's opinions be heard?"

Raoul raised his eyebrows. "Now there's a thought. Maybe some opinions shouldn't be heard."

"Now you're being childish," said Peggy.

"I'm being realistic," he said.

"Decisions can't be made in a vacuum," said Kelly. "That's the point I was leading up to. The task force is going to be marginalized by powerful people who don't want to change the status quo. They're going to make sure any recommendations are stashed away in a file cabinet somewhere, especially the ones they don't agree with. And do you know why?"

"I suppose you're going to tell us," said Raoul.

"It's because there's a lot of money at stake," Kelly said. "Who in this state is going to stand up to real estate developers who want to build condos and hotels on every patch of desirable land they can find? It brings in tax revenue."

"He's right, you know," said Peggy. "We don't stand a chance of being heard."

"You folks are paranoid," said Raoul. "If the task force makes recommendations that aren't followed, then it will be for a good reason, like we've trampled on the rights of property owners. And if you don't think private property is a good idea, then consider the alternative, which is public ownership of everything. Now that's a recipe for disaster."

"I just don't get how someone with your range of interests can be so cold and negative," said Peggy.

"What you are describing as cold and negative is what I call reality," said Raoul.

"With property rights come responsibilities," said Kelly.

"Bingo," said Peggy.

"Oh, brother, now you guys are singing from the same page of music," said Raoul.

Kelly perked up. "Speaking of music, what's that?"

A burst of plucked string music suddenly filled the air, coming from down the aisle.

Raoul gasped. Peggy looked at him. "What is it?"

"A zither," he said. "Oh, my. It's been years."

They listened. The music was calming, and it made Peggy forget about politics and property rights. She looked at Raoul. He suddenly seemed sad and older. There were wrinkles in his face that she had not noticed before. He looked out of the window, either listening to the music or lost in thought, she couldn't tell which.

"What is it?" Peggy said again, softly.

"Whenever I hear a zither, it reminds me of *The Third Man*. It was Priscilla's favorite movie. The entire soundtrack was played on the zither by Anton Karas. We watched it so many times together."

Peggy placed her hand on his arm. She couldn't think of anything to say. He placed his hand on hers.

Thursday, June 23

Ah, Peggy thought to herself, my kind of day. The sky was blue overhead, and to the east it was a mixture of orange, pink, and hints of green. As she walked up the ramp she noticed how the high tide was touching the low-hanging madrona trees that grew out from the banks.

"Good morning," she said to Raoul, sliding in next to him on the bench seat.

As she poured her tea, Peggy heard a loud clacking of high heels. Florence entered the booth, accompanied by a well-dressed thirtyish-looking man.

"Good morning, Raoul," said Florence. "This is Luke. Luke, this is Raoul." Looking at Peggy, she said, "And you are, wait, wait, it's on the tip of my tongue. Peggy. Right?"

"Right," said Peggy. She and Raoul shook hands with Luke. Florence sat with a flourish and crossed her legs. Peggy could imagine her with a cigarette between her fingers. Luke had a tanned, good-looking face and wore a blue suit.

The ferry departed and soon made the turn out of Eagle Harbor. Peggy noticed Mt. Rainier bathed in an orange glow, visible all the way to the summit. Seattle itself, though, was shrouded in fog.

"Luke and I met in a foursome at Wing Point," Florence was saying to Raoul. "My God, I don't know how you guys do this 5:20 ferry everyday. Whew. I'm beat and I still have a long day at the office."

"You get used to it. I like that it's not so crowded," said Raoul.

"Where do you work?" Peggy asked Luke.

"For a small software company in town."

"I wouldn't have labeled you the engineering type," said Peggy.

"Actually, I'm in sales."

"That's why he hangs out at the golf course picking up old ladies," laughed Florence.

"Old? Are you kidding?" Luke looked at her with surprise.

"You are such a dear." Then, to Peggy, she said, "You can see why I keep him around. Every girl needs to have a fan club, right?"

Peggy wondered if she had a fan club.

"I heard a rumor that you two were working together," said Florence.

"Yes. We're on the governor's coastal planning task force."

"They held a gun to my head," said Raoul.

"That's the spirit," said Florence. "I always knew you were a dutiful public servant."

"Ha. That's a good one," said Peggy.

Raoul looked at her. "Look who's talking. I believe you were the one complaining that yesterday's meeting was a waste of time."

"That's because some members were trying to make new rules that effectively limited debate on certain topics."

"Sounds like the other Washington," said Luke.

"Politics is politics," said Raoul.

"It's all over my head," said Florence, opening an issue of *Cosmopolitan*.

"Why does everyone just lay down and take it like road kill?" said Peggy.

"I think it's a generational thing," said Luke. "I was reading an article the other day about how, thirty or forty years ago, it was cool to be broke and homeless. Now it's cool to have money and a nice car and a cell phone. People my age are into having disposable income. That means you go along with the status quo, because that's where the money is."

"I definitely see a change in what young people go in for these days," said Peggy.

"Sounds practical to me," said Florence. She got to an advertisement that had a perfume sample and she lifted it to her nose and sniffed. "Ugh, you could wear that to the Pike Place fish market."

"Young people are smarter now than they used to be," said Raoul.

"You were young once," said Peggy.

"And I was as clueless and broke as the rest of them."

"I'll bet you didn't say that at the time," said Luke.

Raoul cleared his throat. "Let's see, how does that line from Bob Dylan go? '...I was so much older then, I'm younger than that now.'" He sang in a pleasant, husky bass voice. Peggy liked that side of him, the thoughtful part of him that could recite a poem or sing a song and play music and grow wonderful flowers. Yet there was this darker side that seemed negative and cold and uncaring. Which was the real him?

Then Peggy learned something new about Raoul. It was Luke who was speaking. "Were you in Vietnam?"

"Two years," said Raoul. Peggy was shocked. Of course, he was the right age. But the thought had not crossed her mind.

"What did you do?"

"Infantry. I walked patrols in the jungle."

"Awesome," said Luke.

"That's exactly what young people say now. But you didn't say it when you were over there getting shot at. There was a draft going on and everybody, well almost everybody, went."

"But young people now are volunteering to go to Iraq," said Luke.

Raoul shrugged. "Those numbers are relatively small, in my opinion. I think there's always been a segment of the population that is willing to go to war. Maybe it's a patriotic thing, maybe they just like shooting stuff. I don't know. But in Vietnam you had those guys plus everybody else, including the guys who didn't want to be there. And they were all mixed in together. Today, there's about a hundred-and-thirty thousand in Iraq. In Vietnam we had half a million in 1968."

"Do you think they'll bring back the draft?" asked Luke.

"They will if they have no other choice," said Raoul.

"Don't worry, Luke, you're over the age limit," said Florence, patting his knee as if he were her son.

"Of course, they do have other choices," said Peggy. "Like bringing everybody home."

Raoul looked at Peggy, a twinkle in his eye. "Are we going to add the war to our list of things to argue about?"

"Sure. Why not?" She smiled and realized that she liked him even when she wasn't sure if she should.

Friday, June 24

Raoul phoned Peggy at work to say that he thought his night-blooming cereus was ready to open.

"Your what?" she said.

"It's known as Queen of the Night, a kind of cactus. I keep it in my cactus hut."

She had been impressed by his "cactus hut," as he called it, when she visited his garden. It was a warm, dry greenhouse in which he grew several varieties of cacti and succulents. But she didn't remember hearing anything about queens and night-bloomers.

"Each flower blooms for one night around June or July. They have an amazing fragrance," he said.

"I would love to see it," Peggy said.

"Perfect. Would you like to come over for dinner?"

"Sure," she answered, but she wasn't sure at all.

She went over at seven. They had a simple dinner consisting of chunks of baked salmon tossed with spinach leaves and roasted zucchini. He served an elegant French white wine. She felt she was being seduced. She liked Raoul's house with its view of the water, but she discovered she liked it more when Ted and Xena and the others were there. Now it was a little too cozy, too romantic. And the wine was too delicious.

"Let's bring out the cereus," Raoul said after dinner.

They went to the cactus hut and he carried out a rather small potted plant and placed it on a table in the yard. "I think these June nights are perfect. Cool, dry, at least most of the time. I'm guessing it's going to be one of those evenings."

It occurred to Peggy that the phrase "one of those evenings" could mean many things. In an effort to keep the talk small, she said, "How did you find out about these flowers?"

"When I lived in Pacific Grove, California, I had a neighbor who went to New Mexico every year to paint watercolors of desert flowers. The night-blooming cereus was one of his favorites. He would do the painting in the middle of the night."

They drank mint tea and listened to music while they waited for the cereus to bloom. Peggy felt very relaxed. She propped her feet on a coffee table and enjoyed a luxurious view looking east over Puget Sound. The time passed quickly. At one o'clock in the morning they went out to check the cereus. It had bloomed like a starburst beneath a moonlit sky. The fragrance was intoxicating, almost pungent. It smelled like vanilla. Raoul took pictures with his digital camera.

Peggy was truly impressed, but her thoughts raced ahead, to the moment when they would go back into the house, awkwardly wondering what would happen next.

That moment came, just as they were standing around the kitchen, putting things away, the air charged with indecision. Peggy took a deep breath and stood close to Raoul. She was too confused to think clearly and too afraid to let her body do whatever it wanted to do. So she settled for a compromise.

She kissed him on the lips. A long, loving kiss. Then she backed away.

"That was thank you for a wonderful evening," she said.

"Is the evening over?" he asked.

"I'm afraid it is. I'm sorry. A kiss is the best I can do at this point."

He smiled. "In that case I'll cherish that kiss and be grateful."

She gave him a hug and gathered her things, then drove herself home.

FIVE

Tuesday, June 28

"WE'RE COMING TO THE EAST Coast!" Peggy said on the phone to Taylor, Jr. It was a few minutes before five in the morning.

"Huh?" said Taylor, groggy. It was eight o'clock his time.

"Sorry. I couldn't reach you last night, and I'll be in meetings all day today so I thought I'd give you a quick call."

"Who's *we*? Is someone coming with you?"

"Raoul."

"Why? What's up? Are you guys going on a honeymoon or something?"

"Of course not," she said, a little too firmly. "It's a business trip. Raoul and I have been doing work for an environmental task force, and now the governor is sending us to Washington, D.C., to testify before a Congressional subcommittee."

"Cool," said Taylor.

"I'll call later," she said, and dashed out the door.

"I suppose you've alerted the forces," said Raoul on the ferry.

"I called Marjorie last night and Taylor this morning. Taylor was half asleep, poor thing," she said.

"And I called my brother, Dale, in Connecticut." Raoul shrugged. "If nothing else, the taxpayers of Washington State will be reuniting families."

"Marjorie was thrilled," said Peggy. "Did you reach Deidre?"

"Yes. She would love it if we could visit her in Philly."

"I'm so excited."

After receiving the news that they would be going to Washington, Peggy and Raoul had the same idea: turn the trip into a family-visiting tour of the Northeast Corridor. They would visit Marjorie in Arlington, Deidre in Philadelphia; Taylor, Jr., in Brooklyn; and Dale in Connecticut. And then maybe go off somewhere in New England on their own. She was immediately nervous about introducing Raoul to Marjorie and Taylor. But mostly she was happy to be taking a trip away from Seattle.

"Not sure what good our testimony will do," Raoul said, sipping his tea as the ferry made the turn into Puget Sound.

"We've been thorough and balanced," said Peggy.

"Being balanced never gets you anywhere," he said.

"There you go being cynical again."

"It's true," said Raoul. "Who supports middle-of-the-road positions on anything? No one. If you want support for any political viewpoint, it has to be extreme. There's no money in compromise."

Peggy looked at him. "But the facts speak for themselves. We have data showing that a limited amount of smart development is good for revenue while preserving the environment at the same time."

"True," he said, "but if you own beachfront property and you want to build a large hotel that makes more money than a small hotel, then the last thing you want is for someone to come along and talk to you about preserving the environment."

"But if you preserve the environment, you will attract more visitors. People don't want to go for scenic walks in a dump."

Raoul paused, then said, "Depends. If the dump has a go-cart track and a hamburger stand and an ice cream shop, they might like it."

Peggy sighed and turned away. "I'm just trying to give you a taste of what the committee will be like. They're going to grill us on property rights issues."

"I'm sure that between the two of us we'll give them an earful."

"It'll be fun." Then, on a whim, she said, "Does Deidre like art?"

Wednesday, June 29

"I was accosted by well-wishers," said Raoul as he approached Peggy. "It seems everyone who has ever been to Washington, D.C., is an expert on what to do there."

"What have you heard?" she asked.

"One of my biker friends says we're crazy if we don't rent a motorcycle and go touring the Civil War battlefields."

"I got a call from Marjorie, she wants to take us to a photography exhibit at the National Gallery," said Peggy.

"Add it to the list," said Raoul.

Just as they were getting settled and pouring themselves tea, Kelly plopped down across from them.

"I heard you are going to Washington, D.C.," said Kelly. "The seat of government."

"Is that a statement of fact or an editorial comment?" said Peggy.

"Take your pick. But whatever you do, I highly recommend the Holocaust Museum. Have you been to it?" said Kelly.

"My father's side is Jewish, you know," said Raoul.

"I wondered about your religious background," said Peggy.

"We haven't gotten around to discussing religion. We've had too many other things to argue about."

"You can sometimes hear free jazz concerts at the Smithsonian," said Kelly.

At that moment Florence and Luke walked by. "Did someone say Smithsonian?" asked Florence in a voice that was way too chipper for five-thirty in the morning.

"We're going to Washington, D.C.," said Peggy.

"You might catch the Smithsonian Folklife Festival," said Florence. "The food is awesome."

"It will be over by the time we get there," said Peggy.

"Are you going on the White House tour?" asked Luke.

"Oh I did that once, during the Clinton administration," said Kelly.

"It's different now," said Raoul. "You're lucky if you get to see the garage."

"Are you kidding?" said Kelly. "They won't let you near the garage."

"Actually, you can request a tour through your Congressional representatives," said Luke.

"So much for that," Peggy said. "Most of our representatives are Democrats, and they can't even get themselves into the White House."

"That's nonsense," said Raoul. "Democrats can visit between 7:30 and 7:35 a.m. on Mondays."

"Our government *inaction*," said Kelly. "Get it?"

"I'm afraid so," said Raoul.

"When do you go?" asked Florence.

"Our subcommittee hearing is July 19," said Peggy.

"You two should have a swell time."

Peggy could imagine little wheels turning in Florence's head.

"I can recommend an amazing Italian restaurant called Galileo," said Florence. "Luke, maybe we should plan a trip there."

"Sure. Hey, wouldn't it be fun if we ran into Peggy and Raoul?" Luke said.

"That does it, we're getting an unlisted hotel," said Raoul.

"Sounds romantic," said Florence, winking at Peggy. Everyone suddenly looked at Peggy, and she felt like crawling into her tea cup.

Monday, July 4

Fourth of July. Peggy and Florence stood in a patch of shade along Madison Avenue on Bainbridge Island. A parade made its way down the street with a flourish of trombones and sirens. People in front of them shaded their eyes against the persistent glare. Luke and Raoul had gone up close to admire a line of engine-revving motorcycles.

"Luke is really impressed with Raoul," Florence said.

"He's an interesting man," said Peggy. "How long have you known Raoul?"

"I was a secretary at his law firm for many years. We were never involved, so don't worry."

"Oh, it's, um, none of my business really," Peggy stammered.

"Ha. Famous last words," said Florence. "All I can say is that he never looked at me the way he eyes you."

"Come on," said Peggy, trying to sound playful. She had been trying to be honest with herself regarding her appearance. She thought she was attractive, but knew she didn't have the same curvaceous figure as Florence, who was probably a dozen or more years younger. Raoul could obviously date a younger woman if he wanted to. Why would he choose me? Peggy wondered.

Florence narrowed her eyes. "Did you go to the street dance last night?"

Peggy's mind raced back to the previous evening, when she had danced with Raoul in front of the bandstand.

"We had a wonderful time. I could never drag my late husband onto a dance floor," said Peggy, "but Raoul was a natural. You should have seen him move. He's very light on his feet."

Florence nodded her head. "I figured as much. Just take my word for it. He has the hots for you."

They abruptly stopped talking as Raoul and Luke returned from checking out the motorcycles.

Raoul said, "Luke has invited us to go out on his boat tonight to see the fireworks."

Peggy wanted to say no; she had never cared much for fireworks, but Raoul had such an eager, boyish expression that she felt she had to agree. It would be something new. Life with Raoul had been a series of new things, so many new things it made her dizzy. Her life before Raoul had been filled with predictable, safe activities.

When the sun was low, the four of them climbed aboard Luke's motorboat and headed for the open waters of Puget Sound. As they bounced on the choppy waters, Peggy noted that Luke seemed to be in complete control. She had never been in a small boat before, and found it exciting.

At a point just a few hundred yards from downtown Seattle, Luke cut the motor. They drifted, sipping on bottled beer and waiting for fireworks. To the west, the Olympic Range formed a jagged line against a rust-colored sky. Peggy was squeezed up against Raoul on a small cushion. They talked idly about their upcoming trip. Finally, brilliant explosions lit up the night sky with a riot of colors and shapes. In the distance they could see a second fireworks display over Lake Union. Peggy could resist no longer. She looked at Raoul. They kissed while a huge red glow lit up their faces.

SIX

Thursday, July 14

PEGGY LANDED AT WASHINGTON NATIONAL Airport at ten o'clock in the evening. The first sensation she experienced upon walking out of the terminal was intense heat and humidity; the heaviness shocked her.

"What's going on here?" she said to the Sikh taxi driver who loaded her bags into the trunk.

"What do you mean?"

"This heat and humidity. It feels like a blanket."

"Welcome to Washington. What is your destination, madam?"

"Tabard Inn," said Peggy, accepting his lack of sympathy.

Raoul had gone ahead on an earlier flight. Peggy was supposed to meet him at a small, neighborhood hotel in downtown Washington, one they had finally agreed upon after much debate. The Tabard Inn had struck her as an off-beat alternative to the big chains. And Raoul approved of their single-malt Scotch selection and wine list.

Peggy had spent the past several hours on the plane dreading the inevitable moment when she would be alone with Raoul in a hotel room and the time would come to turn in for the evening. After all, they couldn't stay up forever. Of course, she could have stayed with Marjorie, but somehow in the planning for the trip it seemed natural for them to stay together. Besides, it felt to her like their relationship had arrived at the point where they would have to face it.

The tiny lobby of the Tabard Inn was cozy, like a parlor in someone's house. Raoul met her and carried her bags upstairs.

When she entered the room, she fell in love with the soft colors, the polished wood furniture, the bed. In one corner stood an old piano.

"I can't believe the humidity around here," she said.

"We're totally spoiled, living in the northwest," Raoul said. "You picked a great room, by the way."

She collapsed into a soft chaise longue and let her arms drape over the sides. "I'm going to become a slave to air-conditioning."

"Everyone here is a slave to air-conditioning. I don't know how government functioned a hundred years ago."

"Maybe it wasn't this hot and humid a hundred years ago," Peggy said.

"From all accounts, I gather it has always been something of a reclaimed swamp."

"I called Marjorie. She invited us for dinner tomorrow night."

"What would you like to do tonight?" Raoul asked.

He's being so well-behaved, Peggy thought. "Would you mind if I take a quick shower and then we can decide?"

"Not a bit."

She unpacked her robe and carried it with her into the bathroom and then sighed pleasantly as a steamy stream of water rinsed grime and salt from her body. She dried off and brushed her hair. Leaving her clothes in a pile on the floor, she wrapped only the robe around her and took a deep breath before stepping back into the bedroom.

Raoul was reading a book and looked up when she entered. "Feel better?" he asked.

She walked toward him and sat in his lap. "I'm planning to feel even better." Then she kissed him. She allowed her robe to hang open and his hands quickly found their way inside. His touch was warm on her skin.

"What's this all about?" he asked finally.

"It's about getting our vacation off on the right foot. I don't want us building up a lot of tension and stress wondering if we will or if we won't. We're grownups, we're not married, I say we put this hotel room to good use."

Raoul stared at her with his mouth hanging open. She led him to the bed.

Friday, July 15

In the afternoon they drove out of the city to Arlington, Virginia, via the 14th Street Bridge. Peggy was amazed at the mammoth size of the Pentagon as they passed it. Moments later, she had a joyful reunion with her daughter, who lived in an old neighborhood of wood frame houses.

Introductions were made all around. Raoul was a perfect gentleman as he shook hands with Marjorie. Peggy suddenly saw him in a new light; after all, they were officially lovers, and she wondered if it showed.

"I want him to meet Stan," said Peggy, referring her son-in-law.

"He'll be with us for dinner tonight. We're taking you to our favorite Korean restaurant, just a few blocks from here."

"I understand you're a mathematician," said Raoul.

"I do statistics for D.O.L."

"That would be, Department of Labor?" said Raoul.

"Yes, I take it you're not a newbie here."

"My firm has business in D.C. and I've been through town a few times."

Peggy said, "We thought we'd look around Alexandria. Raoul knows a tea shop there. We both love tea."

"It's one of the few things we have in common," said Raoul with a wink.

They left Marjorie's and drove into the old section of Alexandria and parked on a two-hundred-year-old street made of rounded stones. In spite of the oppressive heat, Peggy enjoyed the whimsical detail on the well-preserved 19th century row houses. The Potomac River was just blocks down the hill.

She welcomed the coolness of the Old Town Coffee, Tea and Spice shop, with its walls lined with jars of loose tea and coffee beans.

"This is one of my regular stops when I come to town," said Raoul.

Afterwards they walked up King Street and Raoul pointed out a jazz club that he had been to.

"I feel as though I'm with a tour guide," said Peggy.

"Sorry, I kind of like the D.C. area. It grows on you."

In the evening, Peggy and Raoul went with Marjorie and Stan to Woo Lae Oak, a large, bustling restaurant where they cooked their own food on a hot grill set into the table:

They had marinated pork and beef and many vegetables, including *kimchi*, or fermented cabbage.

Raoul and Stan talked politics and drank Korean beer from tall bottles. Stan was a lobbyist for a media organization, and about the only thing he and Raoul had in common was a fascination with the political process.

By the end of the meal Raoul was saying, "You know, Stan here is pretty sharp for a liberal."

Stan laughed and said, "Raoul is a perfect fit for this family; he has opinions and he doesn't mind sharing them."

Peggy's immediate thought was Wait a minute, I get to decide whether Raoul belongs in this family or not. On the other hand, she was glad to see him enjoying himself. She noticed Marjorie appraising him throughout the meal. She thought, Marjorie *knows*.

Then Stan said, "We have a treat for you guys. This is going to be an awful weekend in the city with all this heat and humidity. It so happens some friends of ours offered us their cabin in West Virginia. It's much cooler, and it's quiet. And you will still have the week ahead of you to do sightseeing in D.C."

Peggy and Raoul looked at each other. Raoul shrugged. "I'm game if you are."

During the walk home from the restaurant, Stan and Raoul fell into a conversation about politics and began walking faster as they talked, gradually leaving Peggy and Marjorie some distance behind them.

"Isn't that just like your father," said Peggy. "He would get into a deep conversation and become oblivious to everything."

"Personally, I think it's a man thing," said Marjorie. "By the way, I really like Raoul."

"So do I, but I'm worried," said Peggy.

"About what? Dad?"

"It's not that I believe I'm being disloyal. Rather, I'm not sure I want to be involved again. Let's face it, it's work. But at times it's nice to have a companion."

"You're not good at being alone, Mom," said Marjorie.

"So where's the balance? How do I find the right mix of having someone and not having someone?"

"It looks like you two are having a great time. Just enjoy it."

"You young people are so optimistic. Somewhere along the way the pessimism sets in and makes us grouchy."

"If you were grouchy, Raoul wouldn't be spending time with you."

"You make it sound like I'm the life of the party."

"You are, Mom."

Peggy thought for a moment, then said, "Try to imagine this from Raoul's point of view. Would he really prefer me over a younger woman because I'm better company?"

"Absolutely. Let's face it, a younger woman is going to be more, um, high maintenance, you might say."

"I see. He can relax with an old lady like me and not have to work too hard," said Peggy.

"Mother! I know you're joking. I can see that smile."

Monday, July 18

As the blissful, love-filled weekend gave way to the week and the real work they were there to perform, Peggy was reminded of the downside of having a lover.

"I'm going to strangle him," she said to Marjorie. Peggy paced the sidewalk in front of the hotel, her cell phone to her ear.

"What happened?" asked Marjorie, alarm in her voice. "You two seemed to be having such a good time."

"That was until I discovered what he's really like," said Peggy.

Marjorie sighed. "I can't believe I'm counseling my mother on relationships. Go ahead, tell me what happened."

"First we got lost on the subway," Peggy said. "We took the Red Line in the wrong direction."

"Happens to visitors all the time," said Marjorie. "It's easy to confuse Shady Grove and Glenmont."

"I wasn't confused," said Peggy. "But he insisted on going to Shady Grove when I knew for certain that we wanted to go in the direction of Glenmont."

"Okay, but then you got it straightened out?"

"Then we missed our transfer. Turns out he missed it on purpose because he had this idea that we would walk from Gallery Place to the Rayburn Building."

"That's not such a bad walk," said Marjorie.

"It is when it's ninety-five degrees and you're in pantyhose and you're going to visit an important Congressman to discuss national energy policy."

"Hmm. Good point. Did he give a reason?"

"He said he wanted to show me Chinatown."

"Not a good choice under the circumstances," said Marjorie.

"Thank you. I felt like I'd been in a sauna by the time I got to the meeting. Oh, and then the meeting. Raoul made such a fool of himself that I wanted to run screaming from the room. I thought he was going to punch a guy from the Sierra Club."

Marjorie sighed. "I'm sorry, Mom. Look, have a glass of wine and get a good night's sleep. Is tomorrow your hearing?"

"Yes." Peggy paused. "Thanks, Marj. I feel better already."

Peggy switched off her phone and went to the bar and ordered a glass of wine. She knew Raoul was upstairs reading. She sipped her wine quietly and then went up to the room. He was already in bed, apparently sleeping. She got herself ready for bed and slid softly beneath the covers and tried to fall asleep. But a certain thought would not leave her mind: Why go through this? I did it for thirty years with Taylor!

Tuesday, July 19

In the ornate sitting room of the Tabard Inn, Peggy and Raoul had their tea while he talked on the phone. When he hung up, he said, "Change in plans. They've tightened security at Rayburn today so there's going to be a teleconference hookup from another building."

"We'll still give our testimony, right?" asked Peggy.

Raoul nodded. "But we'll probably be stuck with that Sierra Club guy all day. He was obnoxious."

"He had some interesting things to say," said Peggy.

"His chief goal was to impress people with a bunch of trivia."

"I see. When you are presented with facts that you can't argue with, you dismiss them as trivia, is that it?"

Raoul groaned. "Here we go again."

When they left the Tabard Inn they walked to Dupont Circle to catch the Red Line. It seemed to Peggy that everyone was very crisp-looking and ready for a day of debating important issues, in spite of the muggy air. She wore a breezy dress with low heeled shoes just in case Raoul took them on another unplanned detour.

As she walked, Peggy felt a resolution forming within her. It started out as a vague concept, but grew quickly into a definite plan as they boarded the Metro. If Raoul did not change his attitude by the end of the day, she was going to leave the hotel and go to Marjorie's house for a few days, then fly straight back to Seattle.

As they rode along in the dark subway tunnels, Raoul said. "You know, I was thinking it might help to give you a little tutorial on how things work on Capitol Hill."

Peggy didn't reply. Her immediate thought was, And I have a little tutorial planned for you.

The hearing turned out to be anti-climactic, at least from the point of view of someone who'd traveled all the way across the country to attend it. A series of people made very long speeches, and in the end Peggy didn't actually get to say anything. The highlight of the day was when Raoul attempted to speak out of turn and was hushed by a large man wearing a suit that was too small for him. Of course, Raoul also had to start an argument with the scientist from the Sierra Club.

Later in the day, Marjorie and Stan surprised Peggy by announcing they had four tickets to a major league baseball game. Peggy declined, explaining to Marjorie that she was thinking of moving out of the hotel and cutting short her vacation.

"But Stan got these great tickets from a friend who's on vacation and he really wants to take Raoul to the game," Marjorie said.

"Can we arrange to give him a seat on the other side of the stadium?" Peggy asked.

"Mom, it can't be that bad."

"You should have been at the hearing. He got into it again with the guy from the Sierra Club."

"Those people can be ornery," said Marjorie.

"Now you're sounding like Raoul. My children are supposed to side with me, you know."

"I am on your side. Look, break up with him tomorrow, but tonight let's go to the ball game. We'll get some Thai food before we go."

Peggy relented. Raoul was thrilled. He was even more thrilled when they got to R.F.K. Stadium and he realized where they would be sitting: third row, immediately behind the Washington Nationals' dugout.

"Wow! What great seats!" Raoul said as they stepped into their row. Peggy sat between Stan and Marjorie. Stan sat next to Raoul, who sat on the end of the row.

Stan nudged Raoul and motioned to a distinguished-looking gentleman in a dress shirt, but tieless. "He's a very senior official at Homeland Security, like maybe number two or three."

"No way," said Raoul. "My firm is trying to win some new business with that agency. Maybe I should introduce myself."

Stan shook his head. "It would be considered bad form. When you sit in the V.I.P. section you don't talk to the V.I.P.s. Besides, that woman with the radio right there is keeping an eye on him. You might get thrown out."

The game went well for the home team. The starting pitcher was hurling an impressive shutout when Raoul suddenly stepped into the aisle and positioned himself facing the Homeland Security official.

Peggy groaned and sank into her seat as she watched Raoul introduce himself. The man politely shook Raoul's hand, and tried to look around Raoul to see the current play of the game. A vendor with a large rack of cotton candy was trying to get around Raoul just as a sweating beer seller was going up the other way. It was at that point that the woman with the radio approached Raoul and asked him to sit down.

Raoul finally returned to his seat at the urging of Stan and Peggy. Two innings later he leaned forward to talk to the government official.

"Our international law practice has a proven reputation in the areas of border and port regulations," Raoul was saying as he offered a handful of business cards. The man's wife looked at Raoul as though he were from Mars.

Peggy said to Marjorie, "I wish I could just disappear."

"He does seem a bit assertive tonight," said Marjorie.

Peggy saw the man nod in the direction of the woman with the radio. She pressed a button and talked into the device. A large man with a bald head and a colorful shirt came down the aisle to Raoul.

"Excuse me, sir, can I have a word with you?" the tall man said in a deep voice.

Raoul looked stunned. "About what?"

Stan looked at Peggy. "He's plainclothes security. Ouch."

"I'm going to ask you to leave the game, sir."

"What?"

"You are disturbing other patrons. I suggest you come with me quietly. The alternative is that we will carry you out. There could be media coverage."

"This is outrageous," said Raoul.

The man talked into a small radio. Raoul, Stan and Peggy turned and saw four uniformed men standing a few rows up, waiting for instructions.

"You're serious, aren't you?" said Raoul.

"Serious as a heart attack," said the guard.

"I'm not moving an inch," said Raoul.

The four guards came down. All eyes were now on Raoul as he was lifted from his seat, protesting, by the four guards. A man with a video camera on his shoulder rushed forward and got some footage. Several flashes went off. Raoul was momentarily bathed in white light.

"All right, I'll walk," said Raoul angrily.

They set him down. Peggy watched him trudge up the stairs. He looked back. Peggy waved.

The government official turned around and smiled at Stan. "Sorry about your friend. Can't imagine anyone hiring him as a lawyer."

"He's not from here," said Stan. "Doesn't know the rules."

"Can I use your guest room tonight?" Peggy asked Marjorie, once everyone had turned their attention back to the game.

"You can use it for as long as you wish," her daughter answered.

The home team won, four-nothing.

Thursday, July 21

"Oh, how lovely," said Marjorie as she and Peggy strolled down a quiet, tree-lined block of N Street in Washington, D.C.

"I love the neighborhood. It's mostly residential, and right in the middle of it is the Tabard Inn," said Peggy.

They emerged from the shaded sidewalk and crossed the street toward the gray stone structure. The midday air was oppressively hot and bright. Peggy had spent two nights at her daughter's house and was now taking her to lunch at the Tabard, a date they had previously arranged.

"Have you heard from Raoul this morning?" said Marjorie.

"My phone hasn't stopped ringing," Peggy laughed. "I'm exaggerating, of course. He called me again last night on my cell phone, late. Then he called twice this morning. He's whimpering like a puppy."

"Has he seen the picture?" asked Marjorie. A small picture of Raoul had appeared in the *Washington Post* in connection with the incident at the baseball game.

"I don't know. The picture was buried in the inside pages. Chances are, no one will see it," said Peggy.

They walked through the tiny lobby of the Tabard.

"Stan and I should come and stay here," said Marjorie. "It's great fun."

They entered a dark room with paneled walls and old paintings and an assortment of sofas and chairs. "This is where Raoul likes to sit and sip his eighteen-year-old Scotch in the evenings," said Peggy.

Beyond the sitting room they entered the restaurant and chose to dine in the cool interior instead of on the patio.

"An interesting lunch crowd, as I expected," said Marjorie.

They ordered crab cakes. Peggy had white wine. Marjorie chatted about her job. "I hardly ever get out for a nice lunch," she said. "This is such a treat."

"You're doing well, Marj. I'm really proud of you," said Peggy. "Stan seems happy."

"I am happy, but what about you?"

"Me?" Peggy sipped her wine and spotted a painting on the wall. "I hadn't noticed that before."

"You're changing the subject. Who is it, anyway?"

"Pablo Neruda. I remember a poem of his that I always liked about old women who go down to the seashore..."

To the solemn sea the old women come
With their shawls knotted around their necks
With their fragile feet cracking.

"I love the imagery," said Marjorie.
"There's another verse that I think about often..."

They come from all the pasts
From houses which were fragrant
From burnt-up evenings.

"That's my predicament," said Peggy. "I have a past. Of children, and fragrant houses, and happy times." She stopped, unable to continue.

Marjorie held her mother's hand across the table. Then they heard a man's voice speaking in Spanish.

Es una copa lleña
de agua
el mundo.

Peggy looked up to see Raoul standing by their table. "That's from another of Neruda's poems," he said. "The translation is, 'The world is a glass overflowing with water.' My grandmother recited it to me often in Spanish."

"What does it mean?" asked Peggy.

"I think to her it meant that there is more life than we can possibly live in one lifetime. There are too many possible experiences. It's overwhelming."

Peggy felt a wave of warmth flow through her. "Can you join us?"

"I don't want to interrupt your lunch. But if we could chat when you're through…"

"Sure," said Peggy.

Raoul left the dining room. Marjorie said, "Mom, you know what your problem is?"

"Yes. I need another glass of wine."

"I'm serious."

"Okay. I'll stop stalling. The fact is, I still miss your father and I'm afraid to get into another relationship."

"Now we're getting somewhere," said Marjorie.

"I mean, I want a companion, but not necessarily a husband, or even a significant other."

"Hmm. Sounds like sex without commitment."

"Well, why not?" said Peggy. "Men have been getting a free ride all these years. It's my turn."

They finished their meal in a lighter mood. Then Peggy walked Marjorie back to her car and said good-bye.

"Thanks for the lunch," said Marjorie. "Are you coming back to our house? Or…" She raised her eyes toward the upper floors of the hotel.

Peggy grinned. "We'll see."

She walked back to the hotel and climbed the creaky stairs to their room. Raoul was waiting, pacing nervously.

"Yesterday I received glaring proof of what a jerk I've been," he said without delay.

"You saw the picture."

"Me and everyone else at the firm. It was e-mailed back to Seattle. At the moment I'm the class clown of Burnett and Edwards."

"I'm sorry. I feel terrible."

"No, no. I had it coming. It's the most humbling thing I've ever been through. I've been taken down a few notches and I needed it."

Peggy sat by the window in a worn armchair. The pale yellow room calmed her.

"You know," he said, "I'm always accusing other people of giving in to one type of midlife crisis activity or another, and lately I've been guilty of exactly that."

"Oh. What midlife crisis is that?" she asked him.

"I'm jealous of people who I perceive to be more successful than me. It makes me wonder if I should have done things differently. Like, live here in Washington so I can participate in the important legal debates of the day."

"You'd live in this sweat box instead of Seattle just so you can exchange hot air with a bunch of lawyers?"

He laughed. "You don't make it sound like much fun."

Peggy stared at her nails.

He cleared his throat. "Peggy, I've decided to leave the firm. I've already given notice."

"No," Peggy said.

"Yes."

"What will you do?"

He shrugged. "Hang out a shingle, find something interesting and fun, perhaps an arts organization that needs legal advice."

Peggy got up and sat next to him on the love seat. "I never thought I would hear those words from you. Is it because of the other night?"

"No, it's because of the way I've been behaving. I need a change. I've been at this grind for too long. It's time to have fun."

She placed her hand on his. "I'm proud of you."

"Let's go downstairs and celebrate," said Raoul.

"And let's plan the rest of our vacation."

"Do you mean you're staying?"

"How did you know I was thinking of leaving?" asked Peggy.

"Just a hunch. I suspect you're the type who doesn't tolerate fools for very long."

Peggy laughed. "We're all fools once in a while."

SEVEN

Tuesday, July 26

PHILADELPHIA WAS SUNNY AND HOT. Peggy and Raoul walked beneath tall shade trees on Spruce Street in Center City, approaching Deidre's apartment. The coolness was a welcome break from the heat and glare of the highway. They had driven up that morning from Washington.

"Don't you love these old row houses?" Raoul was saying.

Peggy noted the high windows and tall doorways and granite steps and caught occasional glimpses into beautifully decorated drawing rooms. She imagined the grand lifestyles that people must have once lived in those rooms.

"These were all family homes at one time," said Raoul as they climbed the steps to a large house. "But most have been subdivided into student apartments."

At the door, Peggy saw a panel of mail slots with names next to each buzzer. Just as Raoul was about to press a buzzer, the door opened. A young woman with green and purple hair pushed a bicycle through the doorway.

"Can I help you?" she asked. Her face was highlighted with bits of silver ornaments stuck into her lips, nose and ears. She wore a man's white U-style undershirt with no bra. Peggy suddenly felt very old.

"We were just about to ring Deidre Stein," said Raoul.

"You must be her father," said the young woman.

"Yes, I'm Raoul Stein. This is Peggy Heggy."

"I'm Deidre's roommate, Dirksy." She looked at Peggy with an amused expression.

"Dirksy?" said Raoul.

"It's an old family nickname. Sorry, I'm late for my yoga appointment. I'll catch up with you guys later." She carried her bike down the stairs and rode off.

Raoul pressed the buzzer, and a moment later the door was opened by Deidre. Her face lit up. "Hi, Dad." She gave Raoul a hug. Then she hugged Peggy.

"Good to see you again, Deidre," said Peggy.

"I'm so glad you could come. Let's get out of this heat," said Deidre.

They climbed an elegant curved staircase with dark mahogany rails worn smooth from use.

"This is beautiful," said Peggy. She guessed the ceiling was twelve feet above the floor.

"It's cheap," said Deidre, opening the door to her second floor apartment.

They entered a large room that in a previous era might have been an upstairs sitting room or parlor. Now it was a studio apartment with a stove and refrigerator at one end, two futons that were positioned as sofas instead of beds, a large dresser, a small table by the window and a tall bookcase. An open door revealed a bathroom with a claw foot bathtub. Every square inch of space was crammed with signs of student living: books, papers, clothes, shoes, dishes, groceries. However, it was tidy, Peggy noted. Deidre and Dirksy had obviously prepared for their arrival.

"This is it, home sweet home," said Deidre.

"One more year of grad school, Dee," said Raoul. "And I think you will find it was worth it."

Deidre said, "Would you like some lemonade?"

They sat on the futons and talked while they drank from wet, cool glasses. Deidre told them about her summer job at a travel agency while Raoul showed pictures from their week in D.C.

"Do you remember the Shrine of the Immaculate Conception?" said Raoul.

"How could I forget? Whenever we traveled, Mother had to visit the Catholic sites and you had to visit the Jewish ones." She told Peggy, "I lived a very confused childhood."

"You were exposed to lots of influences," said Raoul.

"But that's not what got me into grad school. Somewhere along the way I picked up some serious math genes," said Deidre.

"My father," said Raoul; then to Peggy, he said, "Deidre has always been an ace at math. Now she's studying economics."

"That's impressive," said Peggy. "Are there many women in your program?"

"Most women here are in marketing. I'm doing an operations management track with an emphasis in economics. We have two other women, one from Turkey and one from India. They're brilliant."

"We met your roommate," said Raoul.

"Dirksy's a music major. She's the perfect roommate because she spends all of her time at the music building."

Deidre suggested walking around the neighborhood. "I can show you the B&B where you'll be staying."

They strolled through Rittenhouse Square and watched a parade of urban humanity: office workers, students, parents with strollers, homeless people, elderly residents. Then Deidre led them down residential streets with rough brick sidewalks.

Raoul laughed at signs he spotted along the way. "Get it? No park-u-arse?"

"We get it," said Peggy. A block later she pointed to a stop sign. "I like that one." The word BUSH had been stenciled beneath the word STOP.

Deidre said, "That's Philly for ya."

Finally they rounded a corner onto Pine Street, and Deidre pointed out the bed-and-breakfast she had recommended to them. As soon as they entered the cool, charming space, Peggy felt comfortable. A girl played music on the piano.

Raoul made arrangements while Peggy sat with Deidre in the spacious parlor. It was their first moment alone. There was an awkward silence at first while they listened to the piano, then Deidre burst out suddenly with, "Something's been bugging me."

Peggy waited. "I can tell. I've been getting some very intense vibes from you."

"It was one thing when you and my father were chatting on the ferry together. Now you're taking a trip together all the way across the country. What exactly do you want from him?"

After Peggy got over the shock of the question, she wondered what her answer should be. She recalled the evening they spent waiting for the cereus to bloom at Raoul's. He had prepared a wonderful meal, with delicious wine, and good music on the stereo, and was so gracious at the end of the evening when she opted to thank him with a kiss and go home. She remembered how glad she was that she had worn a touch of makeup and an outfit that flattered her. She had been truly wined and dined by a perfect gentleman.

All of this Peggy recalled in a flash, the sensation of that evening, in particular, and the way it made her feel.

"You know," she said to Deidre while Raoul was still occupied with check-in, "there are times when he makes me feel young and sexy. Yes, that's the word: sexy. I'm sure it doesn't sound very noble and intellectually satisfying, but I'm not in my twenties like you and I no longer have your wonderful young skin and your figure. In fact, I never had your figure, and so I don't mind being made to feel beautiful by a handsome man who is interesting to talk to and is every inch a gentleman, even though we do have, frankly, serious differences of opinion on things...please stop me if I've answered your question."

Deidre narrowed her eyes. "Well, he is a gentleman. But I don't want anyone taking advantage of him. I mean, you're a very nice person, but..."

"But?"

"I don't want him to get hurt."

Peggy assumed that what Deidre meant was that Peggy should not even think of marrying Raoul. That suited Peggy just fine, but all she said was, "Thank you for sharing your thoughts with me."

Deidre went home to her studies while Peggy and Raoul continued their walking tour of Center City. In the evening they reunited in fresh spirits.

First they attended a piano recital at the Ethical Society, followed by dinner at the Striped Bass on Walnut Street, after which they enjoyed drinks and music at a jazz club. Dirksy joined them for the evening, at Raoul's invitation. The two young women entertained Peggy and Raoul with funny stories of academic life.

"What's most intriguing are the rivalries between professors," said Deidre. "In some cases you have tenured professors in the same department not even speaking to each other. It's like a sorority house."

"Some students shamefully exploit that," said Dirksy. "But not us."

"We're above all that," said Deidre with a wink.

"Hmm," said Raoul. "I think you'll be well prepared for corporate America."

At one point, Dirksy said, "I understand you guys are going to Brooklyn next."

"My son lives there," said Peggy. Raoul had gotten up from the table and was talking to a musician while the band was on break.

"Is your son a student?" asked Deidre.

"He studies filmmaking at the Pratt Institute, and waits on tables at night."

"Sounds like a hard worker," said Deidre.

Peggy had once wondered how she might introduce Deidre to her son, but now she didn't see them together. She saw Deidre going off to the corporate world with her new M.B.A. to make money, while her son would forever struggle to make ends meet.

Peggy said, "Yes, he works hard but the problem is that anyone serious about art has to make some very hard choices about how they want to live."

Then Deidre said, "I've been thinking about something you said earlier, about how you and my father have differences of opinion. How do you adjust to that?"

At that moment Peggy realized that the subject of her and Raoul probably did not leave Deidre's mind for very long. She chose her words carefully.

"If I were simply joking around, I would say that we are getting over our differences because your father is leaning toward my way of thinking."

"But it's not that simple," said Deidre.

"Correct. You can never count on people changing to suit your needs. It's more mysterious than that. There's either some kind of basic attraction, or there isn't. You can't analyze it, or weigh the pros and cons in some scientific way."

"I think you're trying to say that you can't apply a decision process," said Deidre. "The economists in my department are forever trying to quantify everything so they can arrive at optimal solutions."

"This isn't that kind of problem. You have to feel your way through it."

Dirksy finally spoke up. "It sounds like you've given this a lot of thought."

"The truth is, I don't know what the hell I'm doing," said Peggy. "Right now we're supposed to be on vacation and I'm trying to make it work one day at a time."

She turned to Deidre. "I hope you will at least give me a chance. I would never take advantage of your father. If we reach a point where I believe we could never be happy together, then I will break it off."

Deidre gave Peggy a warm hug. "That's extremely reasonable. I'm sorry for being such a bitch."

Raoul returned to the table in high spirits. "This band is pretty sharp. Hello. Is everybody having fun? It looks like a funeral around here."

The women had a good laugh together.

EIGHT

Tuesday, August 2

A T LAST, A REAL HOTEL," said Raoul as they steered into the driveway of the Marriott in Brooklyn, New York, near the Brooklyn Bridge.

"Admit it, you've enjoyed all of our lodgings thus far," said Peggy.

"True, but now we get an indoor pool, and a bar, and people racing to see who gets to serve us first."

Peggy rolled her eyes. "You're going to be impossible after this."

A uniformed attendant opened Raoul's car door. Another opened Peggy's.

"What time do we meet Taylor?" asked Raoul as they rode up an escalator.

"Around six-thirty," said Peggy. "In the Park Slope area."

"Great. We have time for a swim."

Once they were shown to their room, Peggy and Raoul changed into swimsuits and went to the pool.

"Ah, I've been waiting for this since we left D.C.," said Raoul, after plunging into the clear water and coming up with rivulets trailing down his hair and beard.

Peggy smiled as she treaded water with gentle strokes. She was happy to see him having a good time; she hoped it lasted until he met Taylor. She never knew what her son's mood might be, and she had imagined the worst scenarios, such as Taylor and Raoul getting into a fight over politics.

A couple of hours later, a taxi dropped them off at the intersection of Seventh Avenue and Third Street. Taylor was waiting for them in front of a playground that was crowded with children and parents and strollers.

"Hello, Taylor," said Peggy, hugging her son warmly. He had always been tall, and now he loomed over her. She looked up at him carefully and decided he wasn't getting enough sleep. He looked worried about something. "Taylor, this is Raoul Stein. Raoul, Taylor."

They shook hands. "Good to meet you, Taylor," said Raoul.

"Um, likewise."

"I love your neighborhood," said Peggy. "I wasn't expecting so many families."

"Brooklyn has really become the in place to live," said Taylor. "But of course that drives up the rent."

They walked along Seventh Avenue and down a side street toward Prospect Park. Peggy was impressed with the tree-lined streets and the elegant brownstones.

"I'm ashamed to say I haven't visited Taylor since he moved here," said Peggy.

"You've had a busy year, Mom."

They stopped in front of a brownstone with a small garden in the front. "I have a basement apartment here," said Taylor.

"Are we going in?" asked Raoul.

"I thought we would eat first, but don't eat too much or we won't fit into the apartment."

They continued toward the park, where a music festival was gearing up, then back toward Seventh Avenue via Second Street, finally stopping at a pizza place called Two Boots.

"Best pizza in Brooklyn," said Taylor.

"Exactly what I had in mind," said Raoul. Peggy was surprised; she knew he really wanted a steak dinner at the hotel restaurant. She gave him a point for being a good sport.

"I would love to hear more about your film projects," said Raoul after Taylor ordered an elaborate pizza with artichoke hearts and goat cheese.

"Are you sure?"

"Why wouldn't I be sure?"

"My work is becoming notorious in some circles."

"Taylor, what do you mean?" asked Peggy.

"I'm working on what I call the Melting Pot series. It's kind of a documentary in the form of sketches. I focus on immigrants."

Raoul shrugged. "Sounds like a worthwhile venture. I'm descended from German and Spanish immigrants."

"That was one wave of immigration, mostly European. The country needed people for manufacturing and farming. We wanted them to come. Now we have another wave of immigrants. A lot of Muslims, for example, and people from Central America. We don't want them as much. We don't have jobs for them because we are moving so many jobs out of the country."

"So they drive cabs and mop floors," said Peggy.

"Those are the lucky ones," said Taylor.

"I still don't see why that would make your work controversial," said Raoul.

"Unfortunately, one of my subjects has been arrested for being a suspected terrorist," said Taylor.

Peggy involuntarily raised a hand to her mouth. "You didn't tell me that. No wonder you're not getting any sleep."

"How did you know I wasn't getting enough sleep?"

"I'm your mother. It's my job to know these things."

"How well did you know the person?" asked Raoul.

"I didn't know him personally. I started hanging around neighborhoods with lots of immigrants, doing sketches and stuff, and pretty soon I had a nice series going about a family that was looking for work. And then the cops came to my apartment and they had a photograph of me drawing a picture of a man sitting on a park bench. They wanted to know if I knew the man. I said I didn't know him, other than that he was from Pakistan and was looking for work. I saw his picture in the paper a few days later and it said he was arrested for having ties to a terrorist group."

"Do you think he did?" asked Raoul.

Taylor shrugged. "There's no way of knowing. How can you tell? How can anybody tell? The police are grasping at straws if you ask me."

"This Patriot Act stuff is getting completely out of hand," said Peggy with a worried expression.

"Are the police still talking to you?" asked Raoul.

"They came back a second time and showed me some pictures of other people, wanted to know if I knew any of them. I didn't." Taylor cleared his throat and looked at them hesitantly. "But, uh, I was thinking this might be a good time to take a little break from the city. You know. Maybe leave town for a little while until things calm town."

The pizza came and they dove in hungrily. Peggy deliberately changed the subject and told Taylor about their trip to Washington, D.C., and visiting Marjorie. In the back of her mind she was forming a plan. When they were finished eating, Taylor excused himself from the table.

"I think Taylor's right. He should leave town for a while," said Peggy to Raoul.

"I'm not so sure. Might send the wrong signal."

"I can't stand the thought of him being hounded by the police. Raoul, I think we should invite Taylor to go with us to New England."

"What?"

"He would enjoy the fresh air."

"Fresh air! He might get us arrested."

"He doesn't look well."

"What about us? We won't look well when we're in jail."

"You're exaggerating. He's just an art student trying to get a start. But I'm worried that all of this is putting too much stress on him."

"What about stress on us?" Raoul said. "I thought we were going to have a romantic week in a little cabin on some lake that my brother told me about."

"It wasn't a lake, it was a bay."

"Whatever. I'm sure the F.B.I. will find it."

"Now you're acting paranoid. What's wrong with taking my son on a little vacation?"

Raoul slumped in his seat. "I'm not going to win this argument, am I?"

Taylor returned to the table and took a large sip of his beer.

"It's all settled," said Peggy. "Raoul and I would love it if you came to New England with us."

"Really?" Skepticism was written all over his face.

"What she said."

"Where are you going?"

"We're going to make a quick stop in Connecticut to visit Raoul's brother…"

"Very quick," said Raoul. "He threatened to take us to Hooters for dinner."

"…and then we go to some kind of beach house in Maine that Raoul's brother knows about."

"If we make it past the state line," said Raoul.

"Would you stop being so negative?"

At that moment, Raoul's cell phone rang. "Excuse me." He left the table to answer the phone.

"I don't think he's too crazy about the idea," said Taylor.

"He'll get over it. Besides, I want you two to get to know each other. This is perfect."

"After this he'll hate my guts."

"Nonsense. You guys will eat a lobster and drink some wine and you'll be like old buddies."

Raoul returned to the table. "There's a conspiracy going on. That was Deidre. Her roommate has the chicken pox and Deidre doesn't want to stay in the apartment. She wants to know if she can come to New England with us."

"Wonderful!" said Peggy.

"Wonderful? Didn't you ever dream of having a romantic vacation when your kids were all grown up and on their own?"

"That's so old fashioned. I think Deidre and Taylor would make wonderful company, as long as we treat them like adults."

"Who's Deidre?" said Taylor, looking like the conversation had left him.

"Raoul's daughter. Very smart, and beautiful. Of course, at the moment she hates men because she just broke up with a creep, but she'll get over it."

Taylor groaned. "I don't like the sound of this."

"Finally, someone's talking sense," said Raoul.

"All I hear is a lot of negativism," said Peggy. "I think men become set in their ways beginning at birth. Honestly. Now, who wants ice cream? I saw a nice little place along Seventh Avenue."

Raoul turned to Taylor and spoke softly. "Take my advice: Just go with the flow and say yes to everything."

"I heard that," said Peggy over her shoulder as she walked away from the table. She turned to wink at Raoul, then said, "Oops," as she almost bumped into a casually dressed man wearing a Yankees hat.

Wednesday, August 3

The party set off early after first picking up Taylor at his apartment and then meeting Deidre at the train station. After a quick round of introductions, Deidre promptly fell asleep until they were well into Connecticut.

When Raoul halted the car in front of Dale's house he said, "This will be a short visit."

Peggy was shocked when she met Dale. He was so different from Raoul that she could hardly believe they were from the same family. Dale was beefy and loud in a hearty, back-slapping way. Raoul seemed timid by comparison.

They kept the visit as short as they could without being impolite, just long enough to drink bitter coffee and for Raoul to get a key to Dale's cabin.

The drive was uneventful. Peggy read most of the time, Raoul did most of the driving, and Taylor and Deidre chatted about student life. By late afternoon they were heading north on U.S. 1 in Maine, along Penobscot Bay.

"Could someone please explain what a crab roll is?" said Taylor.

"It's kind of like a crab salad on a hot dog bun," said Deidre.

"What a perfect day," said Peggy. "Look at the deep blue-green color of the water."

"It's perfect all right, we're getting a tour of all the scenic traffic jams between Brunswick and Bar Harbor," grumbled Raoul.

"Actually, I think we missed one when we got lost in Camden," said Taylor.

"But at least we found the refrigerator magnet that Dale's wife wanted," said Peggy.

"She only has two hundred of them, poor thing," said Raoul.

"That crab roll sounds pretty good," said Taylor.

"I wonder if we can get it on whole wheat," said Peggy.

"I think it's against the law," said Deidre.

When they crossed the bridge at Belfast, Peggy snapped a picture of the harbor. "How charming!" she said. "I wonder what people do here."

"I think they all work in a credit card processing center," said Taylor. "I read that some company put one here because there was an abundance of cheap labor, and the people sound friendly on the phone."

When they got to Searsport, Raoul stopped for ice cream at a small diner. They rushed to the bathrooms, then sat around a small chrome-and-formica table and were served water with ice. Raoul and Taylor ordered ice cream and coffee while Peggy and Deidre opted for mint tea. While they were waiting, Deidre said in a low voice, "What a small world."

"What do you mean?" asked Peggy.

"There's a man sitting at the counter who was also in the souvenir shop where we bought the refrigerator magnet," Deidre said.

Peggy pretended to reach for her purse and glanced over her shoulder at a man wearing a Yankees baseball cap. "Of course," Peggy whispered. "He knocked over a display of plastic lobsters that sang an Elvis tune when you squeezed their claws."

"I thought I was being tortured," said Raoul.

Deidre grinned. "Then the lady fussed at him for taking too many free samples of maple candy."

"My, you two certainly are observant," said Raoul.

"I love watching people," said Deidre.

"I like drawing pictures of them," said Taylor.

Deidre looked at Taylor. "Do you think you could draw a picture of my Dad while we're in Maine?"

"Sure. I brought my supplies with me."

Raoul frowned, "I've noticed how some portrait artists specialize in bringing out a person's least flattering qualities."

Peggy patted him on the arm. "Fortunately, you don't have any unflattering qualities."

"At least not the kind you can draw," said Raoul.

The sun was low as they continued their journey around Penobscot Bay. They crossed another high bridge at Bucksport and then drove south to the town of Blue Hill.

"I've always wanted to come to Blue Hill," said Raoul.

"Why? What's here?" asked Peggy.

"A very famous chamber music festival."

"You must mean Kneisel Hall. Dirksy has been to it," said Deidre. "She says we should go to a concert if we have time."

"Let's see what's on the radio," said Raoul, reaching for the dial. "Speaking of chamber music...ah, nothing like a Haydn string quartet with my Maine coastal landscape."

They passed through the picturesque town of Blue Hill and then over rolling hills with slopes of granite boulders and spruce forests that stretched south toward Stonington. Peggy saw signs for art galleries, blueberries, pottery shops, stone yards, jams and jellies, and homemade pies. She began a mental list of things that she wanted to do while in Maine.

"I hope we have time to pick blueberries," said Peggy.

"I'm going to need some directions," said Raoul. "Are we almost to Oyster Island?"

"It's called Osprey Island," said Peggy.

She took out a page of scribbled notes they had received from Dale and gave directions while Raoul negotiated a series of narrow, winding roads.

"When's this going to end?" asked Raoul.

Finally they approached a one-lane bridge with a stop sign. Raoul waited while an old Volvo station wagon came across from the opposite direction. The occupants waved as they passed.

"I wonder if they are the Crannies," said Peggy.

"Who?" said Taylor.

"The Crannies have the house next to Uncle Dale's house," said Deidre.

"I heard they have about thirty children," said Raoul.

"Several different families, all related, I believe," said Peggy.

Raoul crossed the bridge, then drove onto a narrow black-top road. "We're officially on Oyster Island."

"It's Osprey Island," Peggy said. "Don't start making fun of things." After half a mile, Peggy held up her hand. "Okay, turn right onto this driveway."

"What driveway?"

"Right there. See the little dirt road."

"I think that's a footpath."

"It's a driveway."

Raoul sighed as he eased the car onto the dirt-and-gravel surface, then drove slowly down a long one-lane driveway. Rocks crunched under the wheels as they glided beneath a dark canopy of spruce trees broken up occasionally by shafts of yellow sunlight.

"It's like an enchanted forest," said Deidre.

The driveway split in several directions, and Peggy pointed down the middle road. They drove by moss-covered boulders, tall green ferns and fallen logs. After several more turns, they came upon a house perched on a bluff overlooking the bay.

"That must be Indian Cove," said Peggy.

"Wow. We're actually staying here?" said Taylor.

"Awesome," said Deidre.

They got out of the car and walked across a grassy yard toward the house and the water.

"The only sound I hear is the lapping of the water against the rocks," said Peggy dreamily. She breathed deeply and closed her eyes.

"And a slight breeze through the trees," said Taylor.

Raoul shook his head. "I can't believe my brother would consider a place like this. There are no T-shirt shops or restaurants."

"Actually," said Deidre. "Uncle Dale said he got it for dirt cheap."

"That figures," said Raoul. "Wouldn't it be funny if it didn't have electricity or running water?"

"He would've told us that," said Deidre.

"Look," said Peggy, "a lobster boat." She pointed to a white boat lumbering slowly across the blue water.

"Perfect timing," said Raoul. "I'm ready for dinner. Let's go investigate the house."

Raoul unlocked the front door and they walked inside.

The front rooms, facing Indian Cove, were filled with light and painted in soft colors. Comfortable-looking chairs and sofas were arranged around broad picture windows. They explored the main floor and the upstairs bedrooms and the kitchen and dining room.

"I can't find any light switches," said Raoul.

"I think we're supposed to use these gas lamps," said Peggy, pointing to a lamp that consisted of a glass bulb with a cloth mantle in it.

"And there's a gas stove in the kitchen," said Taylor.

Raoul crawled on the floor behind chairs and bookcases. "I can't find a single electrical outlet."

"The refrigerator works," said Deidre. "I hear it humming."

Raoul looked behind the refrigerator. "But it's not plugged into anything. All I see are copper tubes."

Taylor opened the refrigerator, which contained, among other things, several bottles of Geary's pale ale, a local Maine beer. He felt one. "It keeps the beer cold," he said.

"Look, I found the instructions to the house," said Deidre holding up a three-ring binder. She opened it up and read the first page. "Everything is gas powered, including the refrigerator."

"I can't believe this. I'm calling Dale," said Raoul. He took out his cell phone and looked at it with disbelief. "No cell service! Guess I'll have to use his phone. Serves him right, anyway."

"Good luck finding one," said Taylor.

Deidre pointed to a spot on the page she was reading. "Says here there's no phone in the house. But if you walk out to Laughing Lizard rock at low tide you can get a cell phone signal."

"How considerate of him."

"Come on, let's go see what the tide is doing," said Peggy.

They walked out onto the grassy bluff in front of the house and then down a path to a rocky beach. Peggy noticed wet clumps of seaweed strewn over great granite boulders. She pointed to an odd rock formation.

"That looks like a lizard," said Peggy.

"And it's laughing at us," said Raoul. "Must be Dale's little joke."

The lizard was wet and dark. Peggy guessed that at high tide the rock would be completely submerged. Raoul walked over the beach and climbed to the top of the rock, grunting a bit.

"Whew," he said. "I can't climb rocks like I used to."

He looked at his cell phone. "Got a signal!"

Peggy walked closer to the water's edge and slipped out of her shoes and dipped her toe into the clear, greenish water.

"Ooh," she gasped. It was frigid. So much for swimming.

"What do you mean you don't stay here..." Raoul was saying.

Peggy heard someone shouting; she looked up. Several children down the beach were trying to skip stones on the surface of the water. A dog jumped after the stones, hopelessly trying to fetch them.

"Come back, Bug," the child called to the swimming dog.

Raoul came down from the rock. "Are you ready for this? Dale has only stayed here one time in three years."

"Then why is he a part-owner?"

"He said he got a good deal on the house and he keeps it rented constantly, and I'm quoting here, 'to those little-house-on-the-prairie types.' It's strictly an investment."

"We can't complain. He's letting us stay for free," said Peggy.

"Apparently someone canceled and forfeited a deposit, so he's not being as generous as you might think." Raoul looked down the beach at the children. "That's probably the Crannie family. Dale says if we have any questions about rustic country living just ask them. They've been coming here for a hundred years."

"Must be a lot of history on that spot," said Peggy.

Later they sat on the porch watching the sunset and drinking the Geary's. They heard a car pull up. It was the old Volvo station wagon they had seen on the one-lane bridge. A regal-looking, white-haired woman in a sun dress and straw hat approached the porch. She was accompanied by a stooped man with a walking stick.

"I'm Bunny Crannie," said the woman. "This is my husband, Roland Hadley. We stay in the next house over. I understand one of you is a relative of Dale Stein's."

"That would be me," said Raoul. He introduced the members of the group, then said, "Did you say your name was Bunny?"

She laughed a small delicate laugh that reminded Peggy of a fancy tea party. Peggy noticed an embroidered lace handkerchief protruding from the pocket of Bunny's sun dress. "Bunatine is the full name. It was my mother's name. My father was Horace Crannie. We've been coming here for many decades now."

Bunny squinted against the rays of sunlight slanting across the porch and looked at them all very carefully, as though trying to sort out who went with whom, then she smiled brightly. "We sometimes pick up things for Dale."

"Got some screen in the car," said Roland, clearing his throat loudly.

"Screen?" said Raoul.

"For the back door. The last family had a dog that poked his head through it. Dale said you were going to patch it up."

"He did?"

"Of course we'll patch it up," said Peggy.

"Noticed your friend got stuck," said Roland.

"What friend?" said Peggy.

"Fellow came in behind you back there at the bridge. I was pulling over to make room for him and he went off the road. Had plenty of room if you ask me."

"He certainly wasn't very courteous," said Bunny.

"I'm afraid I don't know who you mean," said Peggy. "This is our entire party."

"Roland, didn't the man say he was with the group in the blue car?"

"Yes, Bunny. Sure did. Because we know everybody staying on the island and he couldn't tell us which house he was going to."

Peggy's mind raced. Then an idea popped into her head. "Was the man wearing a baseball cap?"

"As a matter of fact he was," said Roland.

Peggy and Deidre looked at each other. They were thinking the same thing. "Was it a Yankees hat?" asked Peggy.

Roland nodded. "Being a Red Sox fan, I naturally thought it a matter of course that a Yankees fan would drive his car into a swamp. The hat fell off his head while we were getting the car out, and then he ran over it. Guess I would do the same thing if I had a Yankees hat."

Bunny looked at the setting sun. "We'd better get back, Roland. I wanted to get a blueberry cake in the oven before dinner."

Peggy said, "Could you tell us where to pick blueberries?"

"Sure," said Bunny. "I'll write down directions to a couple of our favorite spots."

They left. Peggy turned immediately to Taylor. "Are you thinking what I'm thinking?"

"What are you thinking, Mom?"

"It's too much of a coincidence that we would see a man with a Yankees hat in Camden, and then in Searsport, and now on a tiny one-lane bridge leading to Osprey Island."

Raoul slapped his forehead. "Of course. Why didn't I think of that?"

"Do you mean we're being followed?" said Taylor.

Peggy nodded solemnly. Deidre looked disgusted. "You'd think they have better things to do."

Raoul said, "On the other hand, what can they do here? It's not like the guy can hang out by the drugstore and wait for us to walk by. He's going to arouse suspicion. The Crannies have already noticed him. He must be very inept."

"Let's not worry about it," said Peggy. "I'm here for a vacation and I intend to have one. And if the Department of Homeland Security wants to join me, they can go right ahead."

Friday, August 5

Peggy felt her heart beat slightly faster with each step. The trail up Cadillac Mountain in the Acadia National Forest had been kind in some spots: easy walking over flat expanses of granite, or pleasant strolling beneath groves of birch trees. But those stretches would quickly give way to steep inclines studded with boulders and rocks. Peggy had to choose her steps carefully to avoid twisting an ankle. When the trail was exposed they felt a brilliant sun beating down on them, even though it was only seven o'clock in the morning.

They were also treated to spectacular views.

"We haven't lost the trail, have we?" said Raoul behind her.

Since Peggy happened to be in the lead, it was her job to watch for the blue blazes and cairns of rock that marked the trail.

"I wouldn't be too concerned," said Peggy. "If we get lost we can live on blueberries."

They had been stopping frequently to eat wild blueberries that grew along the trail; it provided a welcome excuse to rest. "As a matter of fact, here's a lovely patch of berries," said Peggy as she plopped down on a flat rock and picked at the low bushes. Raoul, Deidre and Taylor gladly followed her example.

"Mmm, these are so sweet," said Deidre. "I can't believe they're just growing wild along the trail."

"Didn't I promise to take you blueberry picking?" said Raoul to Peggy.

"This doesn't count. I want a couple of quarts so I can make a pie and some muffins," said Peggy.

"Not to mention blueberry brownies," said Raoul.

After several minutes Deidre stood up. "I'm ready. If I sit down any longer I'll never get up."

"First one to the top gets to take a shower," said Peggy, referring to the meager facilities at the cabin, which consisted of heating bags of water in the hot sun and then hanging them from a tree branch. Privacy was not provided.

They laughed, and continued their trek, mostly walking silently, each lost in his or her own thoughts. The hike had been Raoul's idea, and Peggy was happy with him for suggesting it. It seemed to her that he had been trying very hard to be nice to her. His obnoxiousness from Washington had completely disappeared, and she had resumed relations in bed with him after a "period of exile," as he liked to put it.

"I can see the summit," said Peggy excitedly.

Fifteen minutes later they took their final steps onto the summit of Cadillac Mountain. Peggy was awestruck: A sweeping vista of ocean and forests and mountains unfolded before her in vivid blues and greens. The day was stunningly clear. She noticed a family had arrived ahead of them, and couldn't help smiling at the sight of a young girl sleeping on a rock.

"Looks like we're not the only tired ones." Peggy gave Raoul a hug. "This was a great idea. Thank you."

"Thanks for being a good sport. Are you having fun?"

"I am," said Peggy. "If only we didn't have to put up with that Homeland Security guy paddling his canoe past our house."

Then Peggy narrowed her eyes. "I've been thinking of how we might have a little fun with him..."

Monday, August 8

It was a quiet morning on Osprey Island. Taylor sat in the shade of an ancient elderberry tree, busy with his sketch pad and charcoal pencils, producing a drawing of Raoul, who was in the kitchen making blueberry brownies. Deidre was in the yard behind the workshop. She had propped the screen door on two carpenter's horses and was carefully lifting the thin strips of old wood so she could tack down a fresh piece of screen. Peggy saw her occasionally look over at Taylor, as though wondering what his interpretation of her father might be.

Peggy left the yard and walked down the path to a thick patch of young spruce near the shore. She brought with her a battery-operated music player with relatively large speakers, capable of significant volume when turned up loud enough. She also had a pair of binoculars.

Her watch said it was almost time. She heard footsteps behind her. Raoul came down the path.

"Brownies are in the oven," he said.

"Our friend is due at any moment," said Peggy.

"This guy must be a real amateur," said Raoul. "He's been paddling in front of our house several times a day. Does he imagine for a moment that we would mistake him for a lobsterman?"

"Who knows? We're dealing with the government here." Peggy saw a movement on the water, then the bow of a canoe was visible through the trees. She raised the binoculars to her eyes. "That's him. Right on schedule."

The man wore a hat. Peggy studied him through the glasses, and noticed that the hat was new. It had "Eaton's Lobster Pool" stitched on the front. He had been hatless for a few days after the incident on the roadway with the Crannies.

Peggy lowered the glasses. "Here we go," she said.

The music player was mounted on a sturdy tree branch, facing the water. She pushed a button. The sound that filled the air was unlike anything that anyone vacationing on Osprey Island was likely to hear on a typical summer morning.

It was *Athan*, an Islamic call to prayer. Even though the hour was well past sunrise, Peggy had chosen the first prayer because it sounded more dramatic to her. She figured the man in the boat would not know the difference anyway.

The man's reaction was instantaneous. The moment the eerie chant reached his ears he sat up as though someone had called his name on a loudspeaker. Then he stood, causing his canoe to rock. He had a pair of binoculars, which he raised quickly to his eyes and scanned the shoreline and the house while trying to maintain his balance. Peggy had anticipated as much: The plan was for him to see nothing but an empty-looking house and yard.

Raoul had his camera raised and was firing off picture after picture. She giggled. "I wonder what's going through his mind. Maybe he thinks we're holding the first annual Osprey Island Jihad Conference."

Raoul looked at her. "Now I know where Taylor gets it. I can see a rebellious streak in you that likes to challenge the system."

"The system needs to be challenged. It was designed by men. Women can't play nice if they want to be noticed."

Raoul lowered his camera, as though struck by a thought. "Can I ask you a very personal question?"

"Sure."

"What did your late husband think of your views?"

"He was very supportive of them," said Peggy.

Now the man in the canoe was trying to talk into a cell phone while looking through the binoculars. Meanwhile, the canoe had drifted toward the outer tip of Laughing Lizard rock. It collided with the rock, jarring the boat just enough to throw the man off balance. He cried out as he fell into the water.

Raoul laid his camera on the grass. "I'd better check on him." He rushed down to the shore. Peggy followed.

The man waved his arms frantically, trying to grip the edge of the canoe. Instead, he managed to shove it away from him, fear in his face. The cold water must have shocked him, Peggy thought.

Raoul scrambled over the rock and down the other side. The tide was halfway up the face of the rock. "Can you reach my hand?" he called out, stretching.

"My legs won't move," said the man, gasping.

Raoul crawled down the rock. The man was going under. Raoul splashed into the water and grabbed one of the man's arms and dragged him toward the rock. Peggy was there waiting. Raoul got a foothold and climbed onto the rock, dragging the man with him.

"Give me your other hand," said Peggy.

Together Raoul and Peggy pulled the man onto the rock. By this time Deidre and Taylor were on the shore.

"The tide's coming in fast," yelled Deidre.

"Taylor, take the kayak and see if you can retrieve that canoe," said Raoul.

Taylor ran off toward the spot where the kayaks were beached.

"We have to get off this rock," said Raoul. "It's going to be underwater in a little while. Can you walk to shore?"

The man nodded. They helped him down on the shore-side and onto the beach, above the tide line. He sunk to his knees and took deep breaths.

Peggy waited a moment, then said, "What were you doing out there? Why have you been following us around?"

"What makes you think I was following you?"

"Because we saw you in Camden, then again in Searsport, and our neighbors helped you get your car unstuck at the bridge, and you've been paddling your canoe past our house everyday."

"You saw me in Camden? And Searsport?" The man had a dejected look on his face. "I had no idea."

Peggy felt herself grow hot with anger. "Well?"

"I'm doing a favor for my brother-in-law. He owns a private investigative service and he has a contract to check up on people who might have ties to terrorism. But he has more work than he can handle, so he asked me if I wanted to make a few hundred bucks following that guy right out there." He pointed to Taylor, who was towing the canoe.

"Who is your brother-in-law working for?" asked Peggy.

"I don't know. He never says who his clients are."

When the canoe was ashore, Peggy said, "I want you to get in that canoe and go away and not come back. Or else I'm going to call the police."

The man shrugged. "Sorry. It was a lousy job, anyway." Still trembling, he shoved his canoe into the water and climbed awkwardly into it. They watched him paddle away quickly.

Raoul and Peggy stood shivering on the beach. He looked at her. "He could have drowned."

"He should have thought of that ahead of time," said Peggy.

"You were playing a dangerous game in my opinion," said Raoul.

"What would you have done?"

"My suggestion was to simply go out and wave him in and ask him what he was doing," said Raoul.

Deidre turned to go. "I think there's something in the oven." Taylor followed her as she ran back to the house.

"I didn't like that suggestion," said Peggy. "I thought he needed to be taught a lesson."

"Sounds like an emotional reaction to me," said Raoul.

"I didn't stop to analyze it."

"Sometimes a confrontational approach can work against you," said Raoul.

"Don't start lecturing to me. My son's being hounded by so-called homeland security and I'm angry. And this is my way of getting even."

"I can't say I'm a fan of your methods," said Raoul.

"That's perfectly fine with me. I don't need a fan club."

The brownies were burned.

Tuesday, August 9

The party said good-bye to the Crannies in the morning and drove to Portland, where they boarded trains and planes for points south and west. Peggy and Raoul hardly said a word during the long flight to Seattle. They took a taxi from the airport to the ferry terminal and then walked onto the Bainbridge Island ferry. Peggy gazed at a full sky of stars over Puget Sound, reminded of the clear nights in Maine.

When the ferry docked, Peggy and Raoul walked down the ramp. Raoul got a taxi and offered to take Peggy home, but Peggy said she was okay lugging her suitcase-on-wheels up the road to her house. They said good-bye.

She opened all the windows of her house when she got inside and walked barefoot in the backyard to look at her garden, even though it was dark. The dry grass crackled and crunched beneath her feet. Fortunately, her neighbor had watered the garden. Peggy's tomato plants were heavy with yellow fruit.

In the kitchen she made red herbal tea and sat at the table, enjoying the silence.

NINE

PEGGY RESUMED HER COMMUTING ROUTINE and went for almost a week without seeing Raoul. She showed pictures from Maine and New York to her friends on the ferry, and at work she busied herself filing reports about her trip and participating in endless meetings with her boss and staff. She heard that Raoul had been doing the same, and keeping odd hours, perhaps deliberately, she suspected.

But on this particular day, Raoul was suddenly present among the group, casual and relaxed, as though nothing unusual had ever happened between them.

Peggy greeted Raoul politely, then turned her attention to Kelly, who had returned from teaching a jazz camp in Idaho Falls. They exchanged stories about their respective trips. Florence soon joined the group and told them about her new diet. Then Luke arrived, with a new companion. They all looked up, staring open-mouthed.

"This is Paula," said Luke.

Paula appeared to be in her late twenties. She beamed a bright smile at them, accompanied by a polite wave. They introduced themselves.

"Paula just joined our company and she lives in a condo on Bainbridge Island," said Luke.

"Welcome to the island." Florence gave Paula a quick once-over.

"Where did you move from?" asked Peggy.

"I'm an escapee from the Bay Area," said Paula.

"Paula's our newest engineer," said Luke. "She just graduated from Stanford."

"A lot of girls are going into that, I hear," said Florence. "The current generation isn't satisfied with making coffee for the boss and typing memos."

"Thank goodness," said Peggy.

"Florence, I don't remember you making coffee when you worked at our firm," said Raoul, lowering his newspaper.

"That's because you weren't the boss," said Florence.

Peggy gazed across the Sound. The city looked like it did at night: a cluster of lights glowing against a dark sky. There had been a refreshing drizzle when she walked to the ferry.

"The company's growing, but we can't find local people to fill the jobs," Luke explained. "We're having to hire from all over the country."

Peggy noticed that Paula stared at Luke in an admiring way. She wondered what Florence was thinking.

"I thought the streets were crawling with technical people out of work," said Kelly.

"That's a myth. Lots of jobs are going unfilled right now," said Luke.

"Not music jobs, that's for sure," said Kelly.

"How was your jazz camp?" asked Raoul.

"Awesome. I had some great kids. I was thinking of doing one here next summer," said Kelly.

While the others talked, Peggy noticed Florence watching Paula's admiring gaze directed at Luke, and her elegant posture as she sat on the edge of her seat, like a new employee trying to make a good impression. Paula was making an impression on Florence.

"Are we giving you enough room, dear?" said Florence. "I can scoot over." Without waiting for an answer, Florence shifted closer to Raoul, until her bare knees were almost against his legs.

Paula adjusted her position and let her bright plaid skirt drape over her knees.

"Your skirt has a unique design," said Peggy. "Who makes that?"

"I made it myself," said Paula. "I took a design for a kilt and adapted it into a skirt." She regarded Luke with an expression of concern. "I hope it's not too loud for the office."

"It's very nice," he said, with a glance of approval in the general direction of her legs.

"But it's got all those pleats," said Florence. "Surely you didn't do that."

"It took a lot of time, believe me," Paula said. "The cloth came from Scotland. These are my family's colors."

"That's so impressive," said Peggy.

Florence turned to Raoul and leaned against him. "She's a computer engineer who makes her own clothes. I think the younger generation is leaving us in the dust."

Raoul said. "I've been thinking, we've all been working hard and traveling a lot; why don't we have a party? How would everyone like to come to my house this Saturday? You, too, Paula; you're invited."

"She's just getting moved in," said Florence.

"I'd love to come," said Paula with her bright, winning smile.

"Sounds good to me," said Kelly.

Luke and Florence also agreed. Peggy realized she couldn't decline gracefully so she said, "Sounds great."

"Wonderful. I'll give you directions tomorrow," said Raoul. He winked at Peggy. She smiled politely and turned away.

Thursday, August 18

She got a call from Taylor while she was washing dishes. "I went to Philadelphia," he said, and Peggy instantly knew exactly what he was talking about, although she pretended not to.

"Did you have a good time?" she asked.

"Yeah. It was great."

"Please tell me about it."

"I went to an art exhibit. And I saw Deidre."

"At the art exhibit?"

"Yes. Well, we went together."

"How is her roommate?"

"Fine. She's over the chicken pox."

"Sounds like you had a nice visit."

"Yeah. We had fun."

Peggy had the feeling that her son wanted her to know about it but didn't especially want to discuss it further. There was nothing to discuss, really. After all, it was only a weekend visit.

"She's coming to Brooklyn next weekend," said Taylor.

I'm having a hard time with this, she thought. What's wrong with me? "I see," is what she said.

"I'm taking her to an art exhibit."

"I suppose after you've seen all the art exhibits in Philly you would naturally go to Brooklyn. What's next, Chicago?"

"You don't like this, do you?"

"It's not a question of whether I like it. If you two get along, then that's great. Who am I to object?"

"You don't like it a bit, I can tell."

"She's a nice young lady, and smart. I'm sure she'll be a great corporate C.E.O. one day and make millions of dollars."

"Mom, I know your voice. You don't like it. I would like to know why."

Peggy was stumped. That was the question: Why? "I don't know," she answered. "I have a funny feeling about you and Deidre. I can't put my finger on it. Besides, since when do sons listen to advice from their mothers regarding girlfriends?"

"I didn't say I would follow your advice. I just want to hear it."

"I'm glad we got that straight."

"I mean, it's not serious or anything. She likes it when I explain art to her."

"I didn't know art needed to be explained. I thought you simply experienced it."

"That's the ideal, of course. But some people like to know the historical context and something about the technique."

"Okay, so you're bonding at museums and chatting about Vermeer over Thai food. Then what? You know she's on a pretty serious career track. I see her marrying somebody with a Porsche and a really good golf swing."

"I like Porsches."

"Very funny. But you know what I mean. I don't want you to get hurt."

"People don't always think of the future when they like someone. They just do it, and see where it goes."

Peggy had been putting away a tea mug when Taylor said that and she almost dropped it. Maybe I'm too analytical, she thought. I'm dissecting my relationship with Raoul, sizing it up like real estate and trying to make an optimal decision. Maybe it's not that way. But she wondered why she was just figuring that out at age fifty-eight. Perhaps, as a married woman, she had been in such a cocoon that she forgot how to deal with the opposite sex in dating situations. If only Taylor, Sr., were still around. Life would be so much simpler.

"Perhaps you're right, Taylor. I certainly don't have a crystal ball."

"By the way, the other thing I wanted to mention is that I thought Raoul was a lot of fun."

"But you didn't like him at first."

"I didn't like him based on your descriptions. But when I met him I thought he was pretty neat. You have to get past his sense of humor. He comes across like he has an attitude about everything, but actually I think he's very tolerant and understanding."

"Wow. You got all that in a week?"

"We had a few good chats."

Peggy was perplexed and a tiny bit elated. Somewhere deep inside, she realized she liked Raoul in spite of everything.

Monday, August 22

"Kelly, have you finished your new bumper sticker?" asked Raoul as they gathered on the morning ferry.

"Still working on it," said Kelly.

"I must have missed that," said Luke. "What bumper sticker?"

"It reads, *God Created Evolution*," said Kelly.

"You were distracted," Florence said to Luke. "We understand. It's natural among the younger members of the male species when confronted with lovely females." She lightly touched the back of her new hairdo to make sure it was still intact. "Isn't that what they mean by natural selection?"

"It happens among the older males as well," said Peggy, bent over a pad of paper on which she was writing a recipe.

"I thought we agreed that was natural rejection," said Florence with a hysterical laugh.

"I hope we aren't going to rehash that one." Raoul opened his newspaper noisily.

"I thought it was a great party," said Paula.

"How would you know?" said Florence. "I seem to recall that Luke gave you a tour of the beach that lasted an hour. Did you find any new species of evolving life?"

"We searched for firewood," said Luke.

Florence sighed. "I have many fond memories of searching for firewood on the beach. Seems like the best pieces were hidden in some cozy little alcove. But then I always got sand in my pantyhose."

They laughed. Peggy looked up just as the ferry was making the turn out of Eagle Harbor. The lights of Seattle glistened against the dark morning sky; Puget Sound was so calm that the outline of the city was reflected on the water's surface.

"Sounds like you're weighing in on the evolution debate," said Luke to Kelly.

"Since when does Kelly Flinn not weigh in on any debate?" said Raoul.

"Speaking of things evolving, Peggy's turning me into a chef," said Florence. "Are you writing down that blackberry cobbler recipe for me?"

"Yes, with photographs and step-by-step instructions." Peggy scribbled on her pad while halfway listening to the conversation.

"Ooh, let's see," said Florence. She sat between Peggy and Paula; across from them sat Raoul, Kelly and Luke. It was how Raoul's party had ended: the women opposite the men. It was not what Peggy had expected.

"I began the day by picking the blackberries in my backyard," said Peggy to the women, who listened eagerly.

"I think it's key to pick them the day you use them. Don't you agree?" said Peggy.

"Oh, by all means, that's what I always do," said Florence with a wink. She turned to Paula, "I don't think Peggy understood what she was getting into when she agreed to teach me how to actually bake something."

"Perhaps the mint juleps clouded her judgment," said Paula.

Raoul said proudly, "They've been known to do that."

Florence looked at him. "But only to an extent. I would say Peggy and I showed remarkably clear judgment by the end of the evening, especially when it came to selecting things. Or not."

The women laughed while Raoul rolled his eyes. Peggy continued quickly with her narrative. "I picked berries until

I had about two pounds. They were very plump. Look." She held up a photograph.

"Plump and juicy-looking," said Florence.

"These practically fell into the bowl when you touched the bush," said Peggy. "Afterwards I cut up some ripe peaches and combined them with the blackberries until I had about two-and-a-half pounds of fruit. Then I tossed that with a quarter cup of sugar."

"Mmm," said Florence. "It's looking more delicious with each step."

"Let that stand for half an hour, then strain it through a colander. Reserve a quarter-cup of the juice and whisk in a teaspoon of cornstarch and a tablespoon of juice from a lemon."

"You don't use lemon juice from a bottle?" said Florence.

"Never. That would be like choosing second best," said Peggy.

"Second best has a low selection rate. Haven't you noticed?" said Florence with a smile.

Peggy sneaked a glance at Raoul, but he seemed to be focused on his newspaper. She wasn't comfortable with the way Florence was rubbing it in. The whole incident was nothing, really, just a quirky twist of events.

At Raoul's party, Peggy had found herself competing with Florence for his attention. Peggy had known it would happen, even though she didn't want it to, even though she ordered herself not to fall into that trap. Yet, as she'd put on her swishy black skirt and the clingy peach-colored top at the beginning of that evening, she knew she was dressing for combat. Raoul seemed to bask in the attention all night, which Peggy did not find attractive. After all, if two women are going to vie for a man's attention, at least he could act surprised and flattered, instead of smug and confident. Then Raoul stepped on his own foot when he told a sexist joke, which gave the men a good laugh, while Peggy and Florence looked on with revulsion.   It addition to being tasteless, it wasn't even funny. Paula, to her credit, joined them out of camaraderie, and the evening disintegrated into women and men chatting separately.

When they said their good-byes, Florence couldn't resist poking fun at Raoul with dumb jokes about "survival of the unfittest." Now, as Peggy was trying to let the whole episode pass, it seemed she had a new bosom buddy.

"So what happens next?" asked Florence. "Not that I'm going to try this at home, mind you. The kitchen is not one of my favorite rooms, if you get my drift."

While Florence giggled, Peggy read from the page in front of her. "You bake the fruit in a dish for ten minutes. While it's in the oven you make a batch of biscuit dough using plain, low-fat yogurt instead of milk. Also, these biscuits have extra sugar so they're kind of sweet and buttery."

"There's something about sweet and buttery that's so much more appealing than dry and ornery, don't you agree?" said Florence.

"It's a well known fact," said Paula, "that sweet and buttery members of the species have a higher probability of selection."

Peggy pressed on, while Florence and Paula laughed. "When the fruit is hot and bubbly you take the dish out and plop six clumps of biscuit dough on top of the hot fruit. Then you put it back in the oven for about sixteen minutes."

"That's awesome," said Paula. "It sure was tasty."

"Yes, Peggy, it was quite good," said Raoul.

"I like how everything bonds together at the end," said Florence. "It must be the chemistry. I'll bet one dash of the wrong ingredient could uncobble the whole cobbler."

Raoul said to Kelly and Luke, "I get the feeling they're milking this for all it's worth."

Luke's face brightened. "There's only one solution."

They all looked at Luke.

"We take them to lunch," he said.

"Now you're talking," said Florence. "You've just increased your chances of being selected."

"Can we go to Pike Place Market?" asked Paula.

"That's an excellent choice," said Peggy.

"Okay, lunch it is," Raoul said good-naturedly.

Florence nudged Peggy. "I knew we could wrangle something out of this deal."

Peggy smiled. This was a game to Florence, and she was much better at playing it. But it wasn't the kind of game Peggy wanted to play. She wanted to be herself and let things fall as they may. She didn't see the point of "landing" a relationship as if it were a business deal. She decided that if Raoul falls for these kinds of antics, he was not someone she wanted to spend time with.

Tuesday, August 23

Peggy was a little saddened to discover that the soft light illuminating her front yard when she stepped outside was moonlight. At 5:10 it was dark enough for a half-moon to light up the landscape. Gone, she realized, were the brightly lit dawns with blue skies overhead and brilliant orange skies in the east. Winter and short days were approaching fast.

But as the ferry departed and made the turn into Puget Sound, Peggy was relieved to see a smudge of reddish brown, like rusty chalk, in the eastern sky, and a jagged line marking the Cascade Range. At least she would get to see some hint of color on her way to work.

"That blouse looks familiar," said Peggy as she poured tea from her Thermos. Paula's beige top had a distinctive geometric pattern. She noticed Luke being more attentive toward Paula; the lunch outing must have melted away some of the frostiness that had lingered from the party.

"I bought this cloth after our lunch at Pike Place Market," said Paula, holding open her jacket so that Peggy and Florence could get a better look at the blouse. Luke turned his head so sharply that Peggy thought he was going to fall out of his seat.

"But that was yesterday," said Florence. "You made it in one night?"

Paula looked embarrassed. "I get obsessed with these projects."

"That's really impressive," said Luke.

"Thanks," said Paula.

"I'm surprised Kelly hasn't gotten a picture of it," said Raoul. "He's going nuts with his new camera."

"As a matter of fact I got some great shots of the Market," said Kelly. "Here's one of the old produce stands."

"Those stands have been there forever," said Peggy.

"And check out these vegetables. They're perfect," said Kelly.

"When did you start going to the Market?" Paula asked Peggy.

"I moved here when I was in my twenties, to go to college at U.W.," said Peggy. "In fact, I remember when the first Starbucks opened at Pike Place Market in 1971. It was just a little coffee shop."

"That one still is a little coffee shop," said Kelly.

"I'm annoyed that they don't sell the lavender Earl Grey tea anymore," said Peggy.

"Where were you before you came here?" asked Paula. "I hope I'm not asking too many questions. I'm always fascinated with how people get where they are."

"I like the way you put that. I guess we're all trying to figure out how we got where we are. It so happens I, too, was a California transplant."

"Oh, where did you live?" asked Paula.

"Sonoma County, near Sebastopol. My father was a chicken farmer, and he grew some grapes. My mother was a photographer."

"Peggy showed me some of her mother's pictures," said Raoul. "They're quite interesting."

"What sort of photography did she do?" asked Kelly.

"Nudes," answered Peggy.

"No!" said Florence, raising a hand to her mouth.

"It was quite a sensation, even by California standards. She did all of the shooting right on the farm, so I never knew what to expect when I took my friends over to my house."

"Did you appear in her pictures?" asked Florence.

"No. In fact the few pictures of me that I have were taken by my father. That was because my mother refused to take snapshots. She had an elaborate camera for art photography and a dark room, which I was never allowed to enter until I was about fifteen. That didn't bother me; I didn't like the smell of the chemicals, anyway."

"I couldn't resist this shot," said Kelly. A sign posted over some crabs read "We Clean All Crabs. No Extra Charge."

They laughed. "One never knows when such a service might be required," said Raoul.

"Raoul, how did you end up in Seattle?" asked Paula.

"I'm a transplant from Hartford, Connecticut. My father was in banking and my mother was a Spanish teacher. When I was a teenager my father got a transfer to Seattle. I was in high school and I remember having a very hard time with the move. You know, leaving friends and all that. I think big events like that have a lasting effect on you."

"I agree," said Paula. "My father was in the Army and we moved all over. I wanted so badly just to settle down and make friends in one place."

"Of course, I can't go to the Market without getting a photo of the local musical talent," said Kelly.

"I remember him," said Paula, looking at a picture of a street musician. "He was singing a real sad folk song about itinerant farm workers. It was so timeless."

"Maybe we're all itinerant to an extent," said Raoul.

"And I suppose if we could, we would retrace our steps to figure out how we got where we are," said Peggy.

"Or how we became what we are," said Kelly.

"I'm still trying to figure out where I'm going," said Luke.

"Or, do you mean, what you're becoming?" said Paula.

"That's too scary," said Luke.

"This requires significantly more coffee, or something stronger," said Florence.

"Is anyone taping this conversation?" asked Peggy.

"What happens when Fate brings people together?" said Raoul. "Do you ever get the feeling that your path and someone else's were destined to cross?"

"But the timing matters," said Peggy. She felt his attention focused on her. He loved to operate at different levels at the same time: saying one thing to the group, but saying something silently to her.

"Of course," he said. "Think of someone you've crossed paths with. A year earlier or a year later might have resulted in a different outcome, because your circumstances might have been different. But when it happens at precisely the right time...*bang*. It clicks into place."

"I know exactly what you mean," said Florence.

"Yes, so do I," said Peggy. "But sometimes it requires a certain perspective to see it. It's like the forest and tree problem. You have to take a step back to see what's really there."

The city loomed into view. The sky had brightened considerably and now it was a hot, burning orange color.

They had just reached an understanding, Peggy realized. They were taking a step back to see what was really there. And what, she wondered, did she hope she would find?

TEN

PEGGY RECEIVED A CALL FROM Raoul at three o'clock on a brilliant afternoon. Sunlight poured in her office window and she had been thinking of what she wanted to do over the coming weekend. Mostly she was wondering if she should propose doing something with Raoul, something simple, like a walk in the woods.

"I have to go to New Orleans," he said.

"When?"

"Tonight, if possible. Fran's best friend is in the hospital there and not doing well. I've agreed to take her down for a visit."

"How is Fran? We haven't spoken in a while," said Peggy, thinking suddenly of how the beach weekend with Raoul's sister had set in motion a bizarre series of events: the flood, the task force, the trip east, Taylor and Deidre. What next?

"Fran's okay, you know, kind of blue a lot of the time, and now one of her best friends has taken a turn for the worse," said Raoul.

"I see," said Peggy. "Well, that's good of you to do that. Please give her my regards. Should I call her?"

"I'd like you to do more than call her," he said. "I would like you to come with us, if you can get away."

Peggy hesitated. She knew it wouldn't be a problem as far as her job was concerned. The real question was whether she wanted another trip with Raoul. It was one thing to propose a walk in the woods with him, but a weekend in New Orleans was another matter. On the other hand she felt bad for Fran.

"Are we talking about Agnes, the friend she's mentioned often?" asked Peggy, stalling for time.

"Yes. They were college roommates at Tulane. Agnes is from New Orleans."

"I remember now," said Peggy.

"Agnes's family is a riot. I met several of them when Fran took me down there for Agnes's wedding. Seems like a lifetime ago."

Peggy sighed. She couldn't think of a way to back out gracefully. "I suppose I can get away," she said.

"Thanks. Fran will be very happy to hear that."

"What about you? Are you happy to hear it?"

"Yes. Very much so," he said.

Peggy felt a warm sensation swirl through her body.

She broke the news to her boss and then returned to Bainbridge Island on the next ferry. By the time she was packed, Raoul called and said the next flight they could get was at six o'clock Thursday morning.

"I've made reservations for all three of us. We should stay at Fran's house in Seattle tonight and take a taxi to the airport in the morning."

"Okay," said Peggy.

When all three of them met a few hours later, Peggy instantly knew that agreeing to come was the right thing. Fran was very distraught. "I don't think I'll get to talk to her again," she said, sobbing. "When they got Agnes to the hospital she lost consciousness and now her brain's not working at all."

Peggy hugged Fran.

Raoul said, "We'll get there as soon as we can."

Thursday, August 25

They boarded their flight early in the morning, still half asleep following a 3:30 wake up. After changing planes in Dallas they arrived in New Orleans at three o'clock in the afternoon. Outside the terminal, Peggy was almost knocked over by the intensity of the heat and humidity. Washington, D.C. was child's play compared to this, she thought. Her clothes clung to every part of her body.

"Wow," said Raoul.

"Reminds me of Agnes," said Fran. "She flourished in this weather. She used to say it 'envelops you like your mother.'"

Peggy could appreciate the metaphor, but suspected one could only love the climate after a lifetime of living in it.

The sky was blue and the sun blinding as Raoul drove their rental car straight to the hospital. Peggy saw drive-thru daiquiri shops and snowball stands and signs for strip clubs on Bourbon Street. As soon as they stepped out of the air-conditioned car, Peggy again felt the heavy, moist air and intense heat. She could not imagine living in it. The concrete sidewalk radiated heat like a furnace, and there was no relief in the shade of a large crepe myrtle tree as they walked under it. She wondered whether she had brought the right clothing.

As they rode an elevator up to the intensive care unit, Fran twisted a handkerchief around and around her finger. Peggy dreaded the scene that awaited them. She could not get Taylor out of her mind: the stroke, the rush to the hospital; the swift, unbelievable end of a marriage. Fran was pale and quiet. She was facing the end of a friendship.

The scene was disturbingly familiar as Peggy walked through the tiled corridors lighted with fluorescent tubes. Her husband had been taken to a similar intensive care unit in Seattle; Peggy had spent a long anxious night at his side watching him pass away. Marjorie and Taylor, Jr., had arrived too late.

They entered a large, crowded waiting room designed for lots of grieving families. It was subdivided into small areas, each occupied by visitors huddled in tight groups, some holding hands, many with red, puffy eyes. Each group was strikingly similar: young, old and middle-aged people looking as though they were suddenly sucked together in come-as-you-are fashion, uprooted from jobs and distant homes. She saw luggage, toys, styrofoam coffee cups, pillows, blankets, granola bars, raisins, and shoes. Cell phones were plugged into wall outlets, and on a few television screens were news reports of a hurricane that had just passed through Florida.

Fran led them into an area where the bright overhead lights had been dimmed. It looked like a refugee camp. About a dozen people sprawled on chairs and on the floor. A man groggy from lack of sleep came forward. "Hello, Fran."

"Hello, Hulie. Any change?" asked Fran.

The man shook his head. "She's on the breathing machine." He greeted Raoul and Peggy with a friendly gaze. "I'm Hulie Lambert."

"Hulie, I don't think you've met my brother, Raoul. He was at your mother's wedding," said Fran. "And this is Peggy. I needed to have someone with me. I hope that's okay. This is just so shocking. I just spoke to her on Saturday and told her happy birthday and she sounded fine."

A young boy came up with a worried expression and said, "Granny's brain stopped."

Hulie looked at him sadly. "The kids are really confused over this." After a pause he said, "You folks tired from your trip? We got coffee in the little kitchen over there, but it's not very good by New Orleans standards. Whenever you're ready I'll take you to see Mom."

Peggy started to retreat to the kitchen. She didn't want to intrude.

"I'd like to go right away," Fran said. "Can we all go?"

"I think it'd be all right. Jeanette's back there now."

Peggy changed direction and followed them. Raoul gave her a sympathetic look. She squeezed his hand. Peggy felt her heartbeat increase as she drew near the room. She imagined her husband lying in one of the beds as they passed the glass-enclosed intensive care rooms. She couldn't shake the feeling that she was re-living the ordeal.

Agnes lay quietly on a bed, stuck with numerous needles and tubes. Her chest rose and fell along with the clicking sound of the ventilator. Each click was accompanied by a swish of air. Surrounding her was enough electronic hardware to fill a hobby shop. On the pillow near her head were several holy cards and red rose petals. Below the pillow was an old black-and-white photograph of Agnes as a young, vibrant woman sitting at a table and smiling at the camera with her mouth slightly open, as though someone had called out her name in mid-sentence.

A woman who looked exactly like Hulie backed away from the bed as they entered and then hugged Fran. "I'm so glad you could come," she said. Fran's entire body shook as she sobbed onto the woman's shoulders.

"I didn't get to say good-bye," said Fran.

"Nobody did," said the woman. To Raoul and Peggy, who stood quietly at the rear of the room, she said, "I'm Jeanette, Agnes's daughter."

Fran introduced them.

"I hope it's okay," said Peggy.

"Of course. Fran is like family. We're very glad you got her here."

Fran spent some time next to Agnes, holding her hand, while Peggy and Raoul stood back and watched a procession of people. The family members would come and stand by Agnes and cry for several minutes and then go away. Young children were brought in and stood staring, trying to make sense of things. One little girl ran from the room in tears.

There was considerable discussion of whether or not Agnes was aware of anyone's presence. A priest from Agnes's church joined the group and told a story about visiting a comatose woman every day for many days. After she regained consciousness she identified him as the priest who had visited her, even though they had never met previously.

Nurses came in and out checking the equipment and the tubes and the breathing machine. Jeanette led the group in a prayer, while one of Agnes's sisters, Grace, sang a song in a soft voice.

Peggy found herself wishing that more people had been with Taylor at his deathbed, been with her to share in the grief. Taylor was an only child; Peggy, Marjorie and Taylor, Jr., were his only family. What Peggy was witnessing here was far different.

"Agnes had six brothers and sisters," explained Fran. "And each of them had five or more children apiece. You're only seeing the tip of the iceberg."

"It gets pretty hectic when there's a critical mass of us," said Hulie. "Dang near everybody's got to talk at the same time."

Fran returned to the waiting room. Peggy and Raoul followed and got coffee from a little dispenser.

The doctor came in and assembled the group. Peggy heard much whispering and anxiety.

"As you know I've been seeing Agnes for a long time," said the doctor in a calm voice. He spoke slowly so that everyone understood his words. "Although I'm just as shocked and saddened as you are by this turn of events, I can't say it's entirely unexpected. You see, she had a large cluster of blood vessels right at the back of her head." He pointed to the back of his own head. "One or more of them burst just as she was coming in for an appointment. Her blood pressure has been very high, and she'd been complaining of a headache the last couple of days. She lost consciousness very quickly and is not feeling any pain. Her heart is beating, but she's not breathing on her own. We're doing her breathing for her with the ventilator. There is no brain activity after two separate C.T. scans. In my opinion her condition is not operable."

There was silence among the group. Peggy heard the sound of the television set in another corner of the waiting area. The announcer was talking about Hurricane Katrina.

"How long should we keep her on the machine?" asked Jeanette.

"I think we should wait until everybody's had their time with her," said another woman who looked exactly like Jeanette and Hulie.

"Annie is right," said Jeanette. Then, to the doctor, she said, "If we kept her on the machine, how long would she stay like that?"

"Days, maybe weeks," said the doctor.

The siblings looked searchingly at each other. "What happens after we turn off the ventilator?"

"She won't breathe on her own for very long. Eventually her heart will stop beating."

"Will it be disturbing to watch?" said Annie.

The doctor hesitated. "I predict not. But I can't say for sure. You will have to decide for yourselves whether you want to be with her at the end."

The doctor went away while the family members debated what to do. There seemed to be consensus on the key issue: that the breathing machine should be removed and Agnes should be allowed to die. The only debate was about how long to wait.

"I want to make sure everyone is satisfied," said Shirley, another of Agnes's daughters.

"Joe's only been here for a little while. He maybe hasn't been with her enough," said Hulie, turning to a young man reading a book to a child.

Peggy could identify the siblings because they all looked so similar.

"I'm okay, but Rita's in there reading the Bible to Mom and it didn't look like she was anywhere near done," said Joe.

"Well, then, let her read it," said Jeanette.

"How long should we wait?" said Annie.

"I gotta get some food soon," said Hulie.

"How can you talk about food?" said Shirley. "If Rita wants to read the whole darn Bible, then go ahead and let her."

Peggy walked with Fran back to the kitchen and poured water from the tap. Fran gave her some background on Agnes's family. Hulie, Jeanette and Annie lived in the New Orleans area, while Shirley lived in Minnesota, Joe lived in Texas; and Rita, an Army officer stationed at Fort Benning, lived in Columbus, Georgia.

Peggy tugged on Raoul's sleeve and led him out to the hallway. "Sorry. It's a bit overwhelming," she said when they were alone.

"I know what you're thinking," he said. "It all comes rushing back. Your loved one is on the verge of dying, gone forever, and there's nothing you can do in those final moments but watch him or her go."

She saw his eyes were dark and troubled. There was so much that was unsaid between them.

"Raoul," she said. "We've never discussed our death experiences in detail. Can we do that when we get back? I want to know about Priscilla, and I want you to know about Taylor."

"Yes. I think it's long overdue," he said. She hugged him, and they went back into the waiting area.

The family members were huddled in whispered conversation, then Jeanette went to tell the doctor that he could disconnect Agnes. Twenty minutes later, the head nurse invited the group to Agnes's bedside. Annie stayed behind with her young children. Peggy followed Fran back to the intensive care room.

Agnes was now free of tubes and needles except for a single device attached to her finger that measured her heartbeat. The room was silent. She was very still. Gone was the clicking sound from the ventilator. The computer screens were dark and pushed to the side. A nurse monitored Agnes from her station outside the room.

The family members and Fran stood in a semicircle around the bed. Peggy and Raoul stood behind Fran. Peggy could not get the image of Taylor out of her mind. Yet her initial feeling of sadness was disappearing. Watching Agnes die was a reminder that Taylor was really gone. It was so final. The body was a finite thing, and when it was used up, the soul was free to inhabit some other space, such as Heaven, although Peggy rarely used that term since she was not raised formally in any religion — her mother followed no faith except her art, her father had been raised in an Episcopalian family but wasn't a regular churchgoer.

Peggy breathed a silent word of thanks to Agnes. There was value in this, she told herself; there's a reason why I'm going through it. She held Raoul's hand.

While they talked in soft tones, Peggy realized that some of the other adults were actually the grown-up grandchildren. One of them, she learned, was Eric, a young man close to graduating from medical school.

Eric was going back and forth between the nurse's station and the room while everyone stood around Agnes. Finally, Eric came in and announced softly that she was gone. Her heart had stopped. The change in Agnes was not noticeable. She had simply left her body.

The family members touched her arms and hair and said their final words. Rita picked up her mother's Bible and the cards and rose petals and photos that had been laid out on the bed. The nurse brought a small package and gave it to Jeanette. It was Agnes's purse and car keys and clothes. "Oh," Jeanette said, "and her dentures."

Back in the waiting area there was confusion about what to do next. Everyone was hungry. They discussed in great detail who was driving where and in which car. It was finally decided that they would gather at Agnes's house and that Hulie would stop on the way and pick up po-boy sandwiches. He went around with a piece of paper and a pencil and took everyone's order. Cell phones started ringing, as though news of Agnes's death had suddenly spread on its own. Annie was talking to the nurse about papers that had to be signed. Jeanette was trying to get everyone to agree on what time they would meet at the funeral home the next day.

When Hulie asked Peggy what kind of po-boy she wanted, she had no idea what he was talking about, but Fran simply said "We'll take three shrimp, dressed."

After twenty more minutes of discussion, the crowd moved slowly toward the elevators. Peggy rubbed her head trying to make sense of the many threads of conversation that were going on simultaneously: about the food, the funeral, Agnes's car, calling this or that relative. Hulie was not kidding; they did all talk at the same time. Peggy had difficulty figuring out how any actual communication took place.

By the time they all got to the first floor in two elevators, it was decided that Rita would ride with Fran and Peggy and Raoul to Agnes's house. They drove away from the hospital with Rita giving directions. The air had cooled slightly, but it was still muggy.

"There was talk of a hurricane on the news," Raoul said to Rita. "I understand you folks get them frequently here."

"Just about every year," she said wearily. "Last I saw, this one was headed to Texas."

They arrived at the tiny house in Metairie that had been the home of the late Agnes Lambert. Children and adults were in constant motion, the phone rang repeatedly, the television was on but someone had muted the sound. Peggy poured juice into plastic cups for several children. The refrigerator door was plastered with photographs of family members at various stages of their lives. There were infants, toddlers, baseball players, high school prom-goers, brides, grooms, First Communion receivers, new car owners, new house owners. She saw several pictures of Fran and Agnes.

Jeanette looked bewildered as she held up a scrap of paper. "I found a note Mom was writing. It has an address and a phone number."

"And she was drinking coffee out of this cup," said Shirley, holding up a delicate green and white coffee cup containing a brown, sticky residue. "It was probably her last cup of coffee."

Rita and Annie joined them and began rummaging around the kitchen, finding things that Agnes had been in the middle of doing before she went to the doctor's office.

"Do you think she knew she wasn't coming back?" asked Fran.

"We solved one mystery when we got here," said Jeanette. "Her car was parked right out front. She must have taken a cab. She never took cabs."

"And something else," said Shirley. "The cross she always wore was placed carefully on the side table next to the wedding picture of her and Dad."

Fran gasped and raised her hand to her mouth. "She knew. Oh, my God."

Peggy felt a chill go through her.

Hulie came in with a large bag from which he handed out tube-shaped objects wrapped in white paper. The household revved up once again to its previous decibel level.

"Who had the large roast beef dressed? Medium oyster, no tomatoes? Large shrimp dressed? Large shrimp pickles and lettuce? Medium oyster dressed?" He continued the litany until the food had been handed out. Then he passed around bottles of Abita beer to the adults and root beer to the children.

Peggy sat in a corner and unwrapped the paper on her knees. Inside was a small loaf of crusty bread stuffed with fried shrimp, lettuce, pickles and tomato. It smelled delicious.

"Do you know why they call it a po-boy?" asked Annie, sitting next to Peggy.

"No, not really."

Before Annie could continue, a child came up and said, "Can I have ice cream in my root beer?"

"Eat your dinner first," said Annie.

"It's short for poor boy," she explained. "It was originally a working man's lunch. The traditional size was half the length of a man's arm."

Peggy bit into hers and found it so tasty that she devoured it in a few bites. "I must have been hungry," she said with a little embarrassment, but it appeared that no one even noticed because they were too busy eating and talking.

Hulie was trying to gain consensus on a time to meet at the funeral home the next day. Different times were offered up for consideration and then rejected for one reason or another: A certain relative was coming over to pay respects, someone had to be picked up, someone had to be dropped off.

"I need to receive an overnight package," said Joe, the brother from Texas. "We were in the middle of refinancing our house when we postponed the settlement to come here."

"I gave them your mom's address," said his wife, Vivian, who spoke with a distinct Texas twang.

"Couldn't you have put it off?" asked Shirley.

"Now can I have ice cream in my root beer?" said Annie's son, pulling on her leg.

"We lose our lock-in if we don't settle tomorrow," said Joe.

"We'll probably have to sign in front of a notary," said Vivian.

"There's one at Wal-Mart," said Annie.

"Isn't there a Wal-Mart right down West Esplanade?" asked Vivian.

"Can we please talk about the funeral planning?" said Hulie. "What time should I tell the lady we're coming?"

"Are you going to call her now?" asked Fran. "Isn't it getting late?"

"It's an old, family-run operation," said Hulie. "They handled my father's funeral, and my mother's parents', and the funerals of my mother's aunts and uncles. I was supposed to call her at home an hour ago."

"I can meet at eleven," said one sibling.

"I can meet at twelve."

"Twelve-thirty works for me."

"How about two in the afternoon?"

Peggy cleared her throat. "Maybe you should see what time the funeral person is free," she offered.

They all stopped as if Peggy had made a profound observation.

"You got a point there," said Hulie. He dialed a number and went into another room to talk.

Friday, August 26

The group went in different directions. Hulie and his siblings went to the funeral home for an eleven o'clock meeting, while some of the spouses took the grandchildren swimming. The remaining spouses stayed home to receive visitors and packages, and Peggy, Fran and Raoul went to uptown New Orleans, across from Tulane University, to walk beneath the oak trees in Audubon Park. Even though temperatures were in the nineties, it was tolerable in the shade, especially with a slight breeze coming off the Mississippi River. As they walked along a wide path and saw the huge curly strands of Spanish moss drape almost to the ground, Peggy began to feel as if the trip was a welcome and unexpected treat. She looked forward to seeing other parts of the city.

By Friday evening the funeral plans were set: There would be an open-casket wake on Sunday evening followed by a funeral Mass and burial on Monday. Fran told Peggy and Raoul that they could go back to Seattle if they wanted to, that she would be okay.

"Are you sure?" said Peggy. It had seemed to her that Fran was having a hard time with the loss. "We can fly out Monday evening. It's only another day off work. Besides, I would like to see more of New Orleans."

Raoul agreed, and it was decided that they would stay through Monday.

On Friday, after everyone had returned to Agnes's house following dinner at a local restaurant, Rita hung up the phone and said, "Guess what?"

They all looked at her. "I was talking to the Bienvenus, remember Trish and Betsy? Well they said, 'Have you made your evacuation reservations?' and I said, 'What are you talking about?' Turns out they already have reservations at a hotel in Tennessee."

"Why?" asked Fran.

"Apparently there's a chance that Hurricane Katrina will hit New Orleans," said Rita.

Jeanette scoffed. "Of course there's a chance. We're in hurricane season! What do people expect?"

But Rita wanted news. Suddenly the television, which had been more or less ignored, sprang to life after a frantic search for the remote control. They found the Weather Channel and everyone fell silent.

Katrina was in the Gulf of Mexico, still on a westerly-to-southwesterly course. The intensity of the storm was picking up. There was a chance it could be pushed toward Florida or Louisiana by a weather system that was moving north from Mexico.

"When you live on the Gulf Coast, it's like spinning one of those big wheels at a casino in Biloxi," said Hulie. "Those hurricanes could hit anywhere."

Saturday, August 27

The sisters went to a nearby mall to shop for a dress for Agnes to wear in her casket. Shirley's husband, George, went along to occupy the children by getting them *beignets* at the Café Du Monde stand in the mall. Joe and Vivian went to have their document notarized. Fran and Peggy monitored the hurricane while Raoul gassed up the rental car. He called on his cell phone to say that lines for gas were already very long and that anyone with a car should get gas.

At some point Hurricane Katrina made a turn that was more westerly-to-northwesterly. Peggy was startled from a cup of tea she was drinking when Joe and Vivian burst into the house with Vivian saying, "We're leaving on the next plane. We changed our reservations."

"What about the funeral?" asked Fran.

Joe shrugged his shoulders and rolled his eyes. "It's just a hurricane. It's not like it's the first one we've ever had."

"It's coming this way," said Vivian hotly. "I saw it on the television at Wal-Mart. Why do you think all those people were buying every bottle of water and every tank of propane in the store? Do you think they were going to have a barbeque?"

Then Vivian announced, "I'm going to get Jake. He went with Shirley and George to the mall and I can't reach them on their cell phone."

She left the house. Joe stood for a moment in front of the television, listening to the forecast. Then he went into the other room.

Raoul came back from getting gas and slumped into a chair and fanned himself. "It's like an oven out there." He sat with them and had tea. It was relatively quiet for a few moments.

Since the mall was only a short distance away, Vivian returned quickly with their son, Jake. Joe came into the room. "I watched the news for a few minutes and it didn't look that bad to me."

"What do you mean?" asked Vivian.

"It looks like it might hit the Florida panhandle," said Joe.

"Why are you telling me this? Have you packed?"

"I, uh, changed our reservations back to Tuesday."

"You what!?"

"I think we can still have the funeral."

"There's a Category Five hurricane coming! It's going to be our funeral if we don't get out of here." Vivian was livid. "Give me that phone!" She snatched it from his hand and stormed out of the room.

Joe scratched his head. "She's not used to hurricanes."

Then the entire mall contingent returned with a dress for Agnes. The house was crowded again.

"It's getting serious," said Annie. "A lot of people are evacuating."

"Better get gas now," said Raoul. "The lines are long."

"Should we make reservations at a hotel?" asked Shirley.

"Might be too late," said Jeanette.

"We can all stay at my place in Georgia," said Rita.

Vivian returned with a look that caused Joe to wilt like an old azalea blossom. "Now everything's booked," she said, verging on tears. "We can't fly out of here."

"Can we step outside and talk about it?" said Joe. They went out to the patio. Peggy could hear their voices through the walls.

"In the old days we would never evacuate," said Hulie. "We didn't evacuate for Hurricane Betsy in 1965. And that was a bad one."

"Oh no, look at the traffic," said Jeanette.

The television screen displayed video footage of bumper-to-bumper cars stopped on the interstate highway leading out of town.

"I think we'd better call the funeral home," said Hulie. "For one thing, nobody's going to fly in for a funeral with this going on."

Suddenly there was quiet in the room. "When are we going to have the funeral?" asked Annie.

No one had an answer.

By late Saturday afternoon the mayor was calling for voluntary evacuations, and strongly encouraged people to leave. Katrina was officially a Category Five hurricane and the probability of a direct hit on New Orleans was extremely high. To facilitate the mass exodus, all lanes of the interstate highways were opened to outbound traffic only.

But still the siblings fretted. They worried about leaving Agnes's house. Those who lived in the area worried about their own houses and wanted to be around to recover from possible water damage and protect their property from looters.

"How long is the power likely to be out?" asked Peggy.

"Could be weeks if it's a real bad one," said Hulie.

Peggy felt worried as time wore on. She and Raoul were glued to the television while the siblings debated. Suddenly Peggy saw new images of Interstate 10 heading west and what she saw made her sit forward excitedly.

"The traffic is moving," she pointed out. "All lanes are heading out of town. The evacuation plan is working."

They all paused and watched live footage of cars heading west, away from the city. "Well I'll be," said Jeanette.

Peggy said to Raoul and Fran, "I think it would be wise to leave while we can. We can always come back if things are okay after the storm."

Raoul looked at Fran. Fran turned to Hulie and Jeanette. "You won't have the funeral without us, will you?"

"Not a chance."

"Well heck, if they're going, then we're going, too," said Shirley. "C'mon, George."

Rita said to Peggy, "You won't find a hotel for two hundred miles. Why don't you just come to Columbus with us?"

Peggy shrugged. "Sure. If you have room."

"It'll be cozy, but fun."

The house turned chaotic once again as everyone prepared to leave at the same time. Peggy helped bring in patio furniture. "Should we clean out the freezer and refrigerator?" she asked Fran. "I mean, if there's a long-term power outage it will be a real mess."

"Good point."

Raoul found plastic garbage bags and held them open while Peggy started tossing out ice cream, popsicles, leftover fish and old lettuce. She held up a suspicious looking package from the freezer. "Anybody know what this is?"

"Crawfish meat," said Hulie. "Better bring it with us in the cooler."

Rita started going through her mother's cupboards. "Red beans. Definitely. Rice. Coffee-and-chicory. Cereal for the kids."

Within minutes they filled two coolers and several grocery bags with provisions. The rest Raoul carried out to the trash can, which he covered with bricks and pushed against a wall at the back of the house.

By eight-thirty they had formed a multi-car convoy heading west out of the New Orleans area. There were no traffic delays. When the last of the city lights were behind them, Peggy saw miles of open water and swampland dotted with tall, ghostly trees draped with moss. It was eerie and primitive-looking. Fran and Rita were in the back seat talking. Peggy felt exhausted, even though she hadn't really done anything.

"I simply cannot believe a hurricane is coming on the day of my mother's funeral," said Rita sadly. "You can't imagine how perfect that is. She's been in this town all her life, and so were her parents, and their parents, and so on. They all hated hurricanes, but they wouldn't dream of living anywhere else. And now, at last, she gets to miss a hurricane. Because if Mom were still alive she wouldn't be evacuating, and neither would we. And to tell you the truth, it'll probably turn out to be no big deal."

They couldn't make it all the way to Georgia in one go: There were simply too many miles to cover. The evacuation route out of New Orleans took them west on I-10 and north on I-55 toward Jackson, Mississippi. There were state police on the roads, keeping the flow of traffic moving away from the city on all lanes.

Sometime late in the evening Raoul guided the car into a rest stop. It looked like a gypsy camp: Pickup trucks, station wagons, vans and vehicles of all kinds lined the roadway and were piled high with belongings. Peggy saw Louisiana license plates on all the cars. Families were spread out on the grass, napping on blankets or sitting in folding chairs drinking beer. One couple had taken down their rocking chairs and sat contentedly as though they had not left their living room.

The Lambert convoy followed Raoul through the crowded parking lot to a bit of open space on the far side. Rita and Fran pried themselves from the cramped back seat and stretched and yawned. Children took the dogs for a walk while most of the adults limped to the bathrooms.

Jeanette pulled out a cooler and passed around fruit and water and cookies. Hulie made peanut butter sandwiches for the children.

"Do you think we should try to drive all the way?" asked Raoul.

"I'm getting tired," said Jeanette.

"Columbus is a long way from here," said Annie.

"We should at least make it to I-20 and then see how far east we can go. I don't think we'll find a hotel any closer," said Hulie.

After the break they piled back in their cars. Peggy insisted on switching places with Fran so that Fran could stretch her legs. Soon, when they were back on the road, Peggy fell asleep and had a dream. In the dream she was married to Raoul and living on Bainbridge Island. Their children had all moved to Seattle to be near them: Marjorie and her husband, and a new baby, the first grandchild of the family. Taylor, Jr., and Deidre were there, engaged to be married. Then a powerful earthquake hit the region and they all evacuated together to the coast. Peggy didn't mind because it felt so nice to have family around her. They rented a cabin until they could return to their homes, but then decided to stay because they liked it so much.

The convoy stopped in Meridian, Mississippi, and Peggy woke up with a start. The group separated and went toward different hotels. There were few rooms available. Raoul visited two places and came back shaking his head. "They only have smoking rooms."

"Refugees can't be too choosy," said Fran with sleepy eyes.

Finally, though, he found a nonsmoking room and was very satisfied with himself. "Not only that, I paid less than what the other places were charging."

Sunday, August 28

After a night's sleep that seemed to pass in a flash, the convoy got on the road once more and continued east. When they passed the sign for Oxford, Mississippi, Fran said, "Let's stop and see John Grisham. Maybe I can get my book signed."

By afternoon they were in the military town of Columbus, which is near Fort Benning on the Georgia-

Alabama state line. From the highway it appeared to be a collection of strip malls and chain restaurants. But as they turned and drove closer to the Chattahoochee River, the landscape gave way to large, old Victorian homes, some in disrepair, some carefully restored.

"This was once the grand part of town," said Rita. "Now it's making a comeback after years of decline. Frank and I got a good deal on a really large place that needed a little work."

"Is your husband in the Army, too?" asked Peggy.

"Yes. We met at West Point," she said.

"How romantic," said Fran.

"Does he know that more than twenty people are about to descend on his house?" said Peggy.

"I sent him an e-mail, but it doesn't matter because he's out of the country at the moment."

"No place dangerous, I hope," said Peggy.

"Baghdad."

"Ugh. I'm sorry to hear that."

"Comes with the territory," she said.

The convoy came to a halt in front of a large blue Victorian with a tidy yard and tall trees. Inside, the ceilings were high and the walls had been painted bold colors. The hardwood floors were dark with age. It seemed that the first thing everyone wanted to do was turn on the television to get an update on the hurricane. What they saw were long lines, gas stations without gasoline, and a storm that looked as menacing as ever. The large, perfectly formed eye in the center of Katrina gave Peggy chills. It was still a Category Five and was predicted to be deadly once it came ashore.

Hulie said, "Well, I think the best thing we can do is be glad we got out."

"Amen," said Rita.

"And the second best thing would be to take that crawfish meat we brought from Mom's freezer and make a crawfish pie," he said.

"And I'll make red beans," said Jeanette. "I know a recipe that doesn't require soaking."

By Sunday evening they were eating crawfish pie and red-beans-and-rice from paper plates and watching the hurricane news. The city of New Orleans had declared mandatory evacuations but it appeared many residents couldn't, or wouldn't, leave. The mayor opened up the Superdome as a refuge of last resort.

"What I don't get," said Peggy, "is that if they are ordering evacuations, why don't they just get a bunch of buses and drive everybody out? I'll bet there are school buses that aren't being used."

"I'm sure many people think it will just blow over," said Jeanette.

Monday, August 29

The storm made landfall on the coast of Louisiana, submerging the fishing towns of Buras, Empire and Venice.

When the family woke up and saw the news, Hulie shook his head. "Dad took me fishing out of Empire when I was a kid. We went trawling for shrimp in the Gulf, and then we fished for flounder in the channels on the way back in. He was so proud of catching a flounder. I can picture that moment like it was yesterday."

The storm passed on the east side of New Orleans, straddling the Louisiana-Mississippi state line. It covered a large stretch of Gulf shoreline all the way to Alabama.

By Monday afternoon, the hurricane had obliterated the towns of Bay St. Louis, Pass Christian and Waveland in

Mississippi, and had done serious damage to Gulfport and Biloxi. In Alabama it caused extensive damage to vacation spots like Dauphin Island and brought flooding as far as Mobile.

Jeanette's jaw dropped in disbelief as she watched the reports. "Mom and Dad spent their honeymoon in Gulfport."

"My favorite casino is gone," said Hulie.

"I know a lot of people who retired to Bay St. Louis," said Shirley with dismay, as they watched aerial footage of the Mississippi coast showing neighborhoods where nothing was left but concrete slabs on which houses had stood.

But, for the most part, the Lamberts breathed a sigh of relief. It seemed the worst of the storm had bypassed New Orleans. They saw footage of floodwaters, but there was not the widespread destruction that they had feared.

"I'd say we'll be out of power for a couple of weeks," said Hulie. "We can handle that."

"I just hope there's no water in my house," said Jeanette. "The last thing I want to do right now is go furniture shopping. I've got to get my kids ready for school."

The true horror of it unfolded gradually on Monday night and Tuesday. The levees that surround the below-sea-level city broke in three places and New Orleans began to fill with water. Entire neighborhoods were becoming submerged.

Hulie's face was a picture of anger and astonishment. "It's just what they always said would happen. You'd think they woulda fixed it all these years."

The Ninth Ward, Lakeview, Mid-City, East New Orleans, parts of Uptown and many other areas were being reclaimed by the waters of Lake Ponchartrain and the Mississippi River.

At one point, Jeanette and her family sat numb, shocked at what they saw: a video of their neighborhood in Lakeview showing just the rooftops of houses peeking above the water. Peggy felt goose bumps at the sight. Rita rushed to Jeanette's side and sat with her.

Eventually, more aerial photographs appeared on television and on web sites. Agnes's neighborhood had taken in water; Hulie and Annie were unsure about their houses, but in any case it was clear that they would not be returning home right away. New Orleans had become a city unfit for human inhabitants. What's more, the horror and scope of the catastrophe increased by the hour as the thousands of people who stayed in the city were becoming desperate and violent.

Meanwhile, Raoul changed the flight reservations for himself, Peggy and Fran. No one would be returning to New Orleans in the near future to have a funeral.

Wednesday, August 31

Peggy departed Atlanta with Raoul and Fran for the return trip to Seattle. During the long flight she tried to piece together what she had witnessed in the week since they left. She couldn't think about it in any intellectual way. She could only feel gratitude. She was suddenly grateful for the things she had: a home, a job, her children, Raoul. Yes, Raoul. She was grateful for Raoul. She had to dab at her eyes with a tissue. It all seemed so fragile and temporary. So fleeting. Who am I to complain?

They dropped Fran off, dazed and tired, and rode the ferry back to Bainbridge Island.

Peggy said, "I have a request."

Raoul looked at her. She could tell he was just as troubled and bewildered as she.

"Can I come stay at your house for a few days?" she asked.

She was also thankful for the simple answer that he gave. He didn't analyze it, or try to read her mind, or figure anything out.

He said, "Yes. I would like that very much."

They paused at her house in the darkness only long enough for Peggy to grab a change of clothes while Raoul kept the motor running. Every minute was precious.

ELEVEN

Tuesday, September 13

"EXCUSE ME," SAID FLORENCE IN a sweet voice after bumping Kelly's arm as she sat down.

It looked deliberate to Peggy. Hmm, she thought, is Florence after Kelly now?

"Did I interrupt you?" said Florence with a show of concern.

"I am preparing my potato farming shopping list," said Kelly with pen in hand. "Now, let's see, cottonseed meal, bone meal, greensand, kelp meal..."

"Sounds like a recipe for casting spells," said Florence. She sat between Kelly and Luke on the 5:20. On the other side of Luke sat Paula wrapped in a flowing brown skirt with a matching poncho. Peggy wondered if Paula made a new outfit every weekend or if she had a closet full of nice clothes. Peggy also wondered whether Luke had officially ditched Florence.

"...that's the fertilizer mixture," Kelly was explaining patiently. "The cottonseed adds nitrogen, the bone meal adds phosphorous, and the greensand gives the soil potassium. I think my soil is low in nutrients."

"Heaven knows, we can't have that," said Florence.

"When do you start planting?" asked Peggy.

"I won't actually plant the potatoes until next spring. But this fall I'm going to get the beds ready and grow a cover crop," he said.

"What does the cover crop do?" asked Luke.

"It enriches and aerates the soil. For example, there's something called vetch that fixes the nitrogen level to a good point for potatoes, then you just dig it in about a month before planting."

"It's not very appetizing to think of potatoes and kelp and vetch all in the same little garden plot," said Florence.

"Don't forget the aged poultry manure," said Kelly.

Florence's face turned pale.

"I read something interesting about potatoes just the other day," said Paula. "Potatoes are grown in 130 nations and are consumed more than fish and meat combined."

"And they grow from sea level up to thirteen thousand feet," said Kelly.

"And they are high in vitamin C, potassium, and even high in protein for a vegetable," said Raoul.

"And you can get potato salad already made at the grocery store," said Florence.

Kelly looked horrified.

"You haven't lived until you've had potatoes right from the ground," said Peggy.

"Not if they come with chicken doo-doo and kelp," said Florence.

"I visited a farmer once who didn't pull up potatoes until he was ready to prepare a meal with them," said Peggy. "They were so crisp and flavorful that I felt like I was eating a potato for the first time."

"I'll need some help harvesting these potatoes," said Kelly. "One person has to gently turn up the ground with a fork while the other pulls out the potatoes."

"Sounds like fun," said Raoul.

"I'll bring my coveralls," said Florence. "Maybe someone will mistake me for Paris Hilton."

"Who?" said Kelly.

"You wouldn't know her. I forget you're allergic to television," said Florence.

Peggy turned to Raoul. "Doesn't Kelly's project sound interesting? Maybe we should plant something."

Before Raoul could answer, Florence said, "Planning to put down roots over there, are you?"

Peggy turned pink. "It's just a garden."

Raoul came to her rescue. "What would you like to plant?"

"Why don't we plant something that goes with potatoes?" she suggested. "Then we can have a grand feast next summer."

"Great idea," said Kelly. "I'm planting Ruby Crescents, which are very versatile, and, if it works, a potato called Rose Fir, a cream-colored fingerling with a nutty flavor."

"Maybe we should grow a variety of green vegetables," said Peggy.

"That's a lovely idea," said Florence. "I'll bring steak. Luke and Paula, are you two planning to grow anything?"

Paula looked at Luke. "I've always wanted to make wine," she said.

"Sure, I love wine," said Luke, who seemed as if he was struggling to comprehend what Florence was really talking about.

"Are you sure you don't want to think it over?" said Florence. "It could be a long-term effort, you know."

Luke tried to appear more confident. "I think I'm up for it."

Florence sighed. "Seems everybody's got a new hobby these days."

"I'm supposed to teach you to cook," said Peggy. "You told me you wanted to try something after I gave you that cobbler recipe."

"Do you know what my kitchen is? It's an unwrapping room."

"We'll start with something simple. Let's do it this weekend," said Peggy.

"What the heck, I'll give it a whirl," said Florence.

"That's the spirit," said Raoul.

Peggy looked out at the dark morning over Puget Sound and saw the reflection of the group in the ferry window. The faces were in shadow, but smiling. She was reminded of a painting by Van Gogh, *The Potato Eaters*. What once struck her about the painting was how it depicted a family drawing comfort from very small things: a meal of potatoes, a single light over the table, the company of others.

Wednesday, September 14

Ever since New Orleans, Peggy had been basking in the glow of warmth and companionship from Raoul. The past was forgotten; whatever misgivings she had had about him disappeared in a blur of frenzied lovemaking.

Living together entailed a different routine for both of them. Before moving in with Raoul, Peggy had had a ten-minute walk to the ferry, and Raoul had ridden his motorcycle. Now they both rode in his car from his house near the Rolling Bay area of Bainbridge Island. He didn't like driving the car: It was more expensive to take on the ferry than a motorcycle, and you had to wait longer to get on.

But Raoul didn't complain, and Peggy silently thanked him for that. She once offered to ride with him on the motorcycle; in fact she had tried to insist. But something in her voice must have betrayed her because he rejected the idea saying, "I can't picture you on the back of a motorcycle at five o'clock in the morning." He was right; it was not her.

On this day, as they rode past the silent, dark forest in the direction of the ferry terminal, Peggy reflected on how she was filling a vacant space left in Raoul's house by his late wife. It had been seven years, yet her absence was still noticeable. It looked as if the house had another occupant who was away on a trip. In the meantime, Peggy was using her sink, and hanging clothes in her closet, and sitting in her chair at the table, and sleeping on her side of the bed. True, Raoul had made a gallant effort to make way for Peggy. He cleared his late wife's bathroom things away from the sink; he moved most, but not all, of her clothes out of the closet. He had left two long dresses that, to Peggy, said volumes about Priscilla. They were fashionable, and sized for a tall, slender woman. Priscilla had been a dancer and actor, and was good at fundraising for charitable causes. Peggy could picture her working a room in these dresses, glamorous and confident. What man with a checkbook would be able to resist?

Peggy was different from Priscilla, and Raoul was different from Taylor. She had to admit they were each compromising a little bit, accepting someone new and different.

Peggy was shocked to realize that she had been at Raoul's house for almost two weeks. She had gone back to her own place a few times to get mail and rotate her clothing so she wasn't wearing the same things all the time. She wondered how long she was going to do this. I haven't exactly moved in, she thought. But, on the other hand, I'm in no hurry to go back.

As they waited in line and then drove on to the ferry, she wondered if she wanted to move in with him permanently. Did she want to marry him? Or did she want to go back to her place and have an indefinite dating relationship? And what about him? What did he want? He could decide that he would rather be alone, she realized.

As so often happened, it was Florence who voiced Peggy's thoughts.

"I can't decide whether I prefer to live alone or with someone," said Florence, seemingly out of nowhere, although, with her, every utterance had a purpose, and a target.

"You should live alone," said Paula confidently. Luke looked at her with surprise.

"And why is that?" said Florence.

"Because then you're in control, and you have time for your hobbies," said Paula.

"But I'm in control now and it doesn't make me happy. And besides, I don't have any hobbies," said Florence.

"That's where women go wrong, in my opinion," said Paula, who wore a plaid skirt that Peggy had seen before, but this time it was matched with a different vest and dark hose. "They depend on some man to make them happy. Forget it. You have to make yourself happy."

Now Luke looked truly astonished. Peggy had to hide her grin. She tried to imagine Luke's point of view. Perhaps Paula was younger and more beautiful than Florence, but Florence was a traditionalist and didn't mind pampering a man.

"Suppose two people each have their own hobbies and interests," said Peggy. "Then you can have a little bit of both. You do your own things, but at times you do things together."

Paula said, "I haven't met many men my age who want that. They want somebody to take care of the home front while they go off and become successful."

"It's true," said Peggy. "I suppose priorities change at different stages of life. When my children were young, I certainly had different priorities than I do now."

"But it's not all as you say," said Florence. "Some of the younger girls in my office can't wait to find a husband and quit working. They would much rather be at home walking the dog and shopping."

"Unfortunately, there are those who give my age group a bad name," said Paula.

Meanwhile, Raoul had shared his newspaper with Kelly and they sat silently absorbed in the pages. Luke, however, was stuck between Florence and Paula and seemed as if he wanted to disappear behind something, anything.

But then Raoul said, "Florence, you are going to have a hobby. Peggy's going to teach you to make shrimp stew."

"Huh?" said Florence.

"Yes, I meant to tell you that I got this great recipe from the family we visited in New Orleans," said Peggy. "Why don't we learn it together?"

"You don't know what you're getting into," said Florence.

"It'll be fun. You don't mind peeling shrimp, do you?" said Peggy.

"You mean they aren't frozen?"

"Nope. We're starting from scratch."

"Remind me to bring gloves," Florence said.

Raoul closed his paper with an air of things being settled. "In that case, dinner at my house. Everyone's invited."

"But wait," said Peggy. "Let's try not to gang up on the host this time."

Florence cleared her throat. "Peggy, you are the host."

Peggy turned red. It was as if her life had gone off in its own direction without her having willed it. Who's in charge here?

Saturday, September 17

"Shrimp stew. 'From the kitchen of Agnes Lambert.'" Florence said the words aloud as she read them from the handwritten recipe.

They were gathered at Raoul's house. Peggy and Florence stood at the counter wearing aprons while Luke and Raoul drank wine near the fireplace.

"What's wrong with this picture?" said Florence, nodding toward the men.

"Let them be blissfully ignorant," said Peggy. "Now let's see, first we peel the shrimp."

"I was afraid you'd say that," said Florence.

"I read Agnes's notes on this, which were given to me by Fran," said Peggy. "Agnes swears by medium Gulf shrimp. On Bainbridge Island you can get them at the Town and Country market."

They stood at the sink and peeled shrimp, with Florence making faces.

"Then we make a roux," said Peggy.

"That's equal parts flour and oil," said Florence.

"Bravo. We'll go with her suggestion of 3 tablespoons of each," said Peggy.

"You'll have to demonstrate this technique," said Florence.

"You start with a heavy pot and get it warmed up on medium heat," Peggy said. "This cast iron Dutch oven of Raoul's is perfect."

Then she continued, "When the pot is warm you add the oil and let it get hot. Then you add the flour slowly, stirring constantly with a big wooden spoon."

Peggy stirred rapidly.

"The roux will be white at first, but as the flour cooks it will turn brown. You want it to be the color of cardboard. Those are her words."

Peggy watched the roux carefully as she stirred. "When the roux is the right color, we add the shrimp and toss them around until they are good and coated with the roux. Then we add a kettle of hot water."

"Which we have simmering right here," said Florence. "My, this is fun."

"Now we add half of a bell pepper, a stalk of celery cut in half, and half of a small onion. All of these are placed in the pot whole. You don't chop them."

Peggy consulted the recipe. "Then we add, and I'm quoting, 'a dash of Lea & Perrins, some dried parsley, salt and pepper.'"

"Is that Worcestershire sauce?" asked Florence.

"Yes. Let's try a teaspoon of the Lea & Perrins and a tablespoon of the parsley. Go easy on the salt and pepper at first."

Florence added the ingredients.

"Then we cook it for about an hour. When we're about halfway through, let's start some white rice. Fran told me that Agnes only used Uncle Ben's."

"She sure was particular about her ingredients," said Florence.

"I gathered as much from Fran. We're supposed to serve the stew over the rice, and have it with lima beans or green beans on the side," added Peggy.

"Don't forget to cut up a nice fresh baguette to go with that," said Luke from the living room.

"You know, you guys could get in here and do some work," said Florence. "You'd think this was the Jackie Gleason show or something."

Luke and Raoul came into the kitchen and sniffed the air hungrily and began cutting bread. Kelly showed up, and soon Paula did, too. Florence put them all to work setting the table for dinner. Peggy observed that Florence enjoyed playing host; she could easily imagine Florence living with Raoul, and she could imagine Raoul being very comfortable with Florence. Peggy suspected that what Raoul really wanted at this point in his life was a new permanent partner. Peggy couldn't decide if *partner* was the right word for what she wanted.

Finally, dinner was served. Voices were raised in a chorus of oohs and ahs.

Raoul proposed a toast, "To the kitchen of Agnes Lambert."

"To the kitchens of all New Orleans chefs," said Peggy.

"Cheers!" Their glasses clinked in unison.

Saturday, September 24

A week later, Peggy and Raoul hosted another party. Raoul invited his musician friends over to work on song lyrics for a contest being held by a local radio station. Peggy had met them at previous gatherings. There was Ted, on lute, and Xena, the viola da gamba player. Xena's granddaughter, Laura, was there with her bass recorder, and Raoul had his alto recorder.

"You guys aren't being very creative," Raoul complained after they had played for a while. "If we're going to win this contest we need more color."

Peggy sipped a glass of red wine with her legs curled beneath her on the floor. Outside, on a wet Sunday afternoon, autumn leaves careened through the air and splattered against the windows, decorating the glass with dots of gold, red and brown. A small fire burned in the wood stove.

"Raoul, maybe you should play the recording again," said Laura. "We might be inspired."

"Maybe you should serve more wine," said Xena, peering into her empty glass.

Peggy passed a bottle of rioja to Xena. As she poured, the stream of dark wine threw off a deep purple tint as it splashed into her glass. Peggy loved that color of wine, it was a rich, youthful hue, an indication of great promise.

"Okay, here's Ella Fitzgerald singing the famous Cole Porter song, 'Let's Do It.'" Raoul pushed a button on his stereo. "Could we all pay attention this time?"

"Give that man some wine," said Xena.

The contest was to see who could come up with the best new verses to "Let's Do It." Five entries were going to be selected and sung on the radio by a professional jazz singer.

As Peggy listened, a thought came to her and she began to scribble on a pad. When the music was over she cleared her throat.

"How does this sound? I can't sing of course, but it would go something like this..."

'Roos in zoos do it
Maybe in twos with kazoos they do it.
Let's do it. Let's fall in love.

"I love it," said Raoul.

Xena swallowed a sip of wine hurriedly. "Wait, you just inspired me. How about this..." With a lilting, husky voice she sang:

In Kentucky they race to it.
With a mint julep or three they brace through it.
Let's do it. Let's fall in love.

Ted frowned. "I don't know if my lute can do it."

"Of course it can," said Peggy. "If you can."

Ted blushed and started plucking and stretching the strings to find those in-between notes that no renaissance lute player would dream of looking for. But then again, thought Peggy, we weren't there.

Raoul looked at his watch. "What's keeping Kelly? I need his warped sense of humor at a time like this."

Laura raised a piece of paper timidly. "This is so silly, but here goes..."

Crusty crustaceans and their pals do it.
Even croaking frogs hop to it.
Let's do it. Let's fall in love.

"It'll work," said Raoul. "With this audience you've got to get in the environmental aspect."

"What's going on here?" Kelly entered the room, carrying a worn black case. "I had to let myself in because no one answered the door."

Xena handed him the rioja. "I'm Xena. Have some wine and put on your thinking cap."

"Can I take out my trumpet? I heard there was going to be music," said Kelly, reaching for a glass. "I'm Kelly Flinn." He and Xena shook hands; lingering, Peggy noticed, just a tiny fraction of a second longer than necessary. Then Raoul introduced Kelly to the others.

"Yes, we need your horn," said Raoul. He explained the project and played the Ella Fitzgerald recording for the fourth time.

"Ah, yes, a classic tune," said Kelly. He pulled a shiny but well-used trumpet from its case. "Hmm. Wait. Wait. Something comes to mind. You know me, I can't resist the political angle."

He set his instrument down and accepted a piece of paper and a pen that Xena handed to him. Then he wrote some words quickly.

"I will not volunteer to sing this," said Kelly, holding up the page. "But I'll be happy to play along."

"I'll see if I can make something of it," said Xena. Ted provided a rhythmic accompaniment on lute while Laura laid down a bluesy bass line on her recorder. Raoul chimed in with his alto recorder. Kelly blew warm, soft tones on a muted trumpet. To Peggy's ears they started to sound like a real jazz band.

In the Senate they call the roll.
The White House likes to take a poll.

Eventually they resolve to do it. Or not.
Let's do it. Let's fall in love.

Everyone had a good laugh. "I knew Kel would come through," said Raoul.

"It's my natural cynicism," said Kelly.

"I think we need to record this while our inhibitions are down," said Peggy. She got a blank tape loaded while Raoul positioned a microphone. Xena sang through all the verses while the musicians varied the accompaniment and worked in a few solos. Peggy sat on the floor and provided an audience. She noticed that Kelly seemed mesmerized with Xena's singing, and when Kelly played, Xena stared dreamily.

"You have a great ear for improvisation," said Xena to Kelly later while they helped themselves to food and wine.

"Thanks. My horn goes well with your voice, which has a very warm quality to it," said Kelly.

Xena sighed. "It was a different voice thirty years ago."

"It has aged well," said Kelly.

Peggy served herself goat cheese and rice crackers topped with bits of smoked salmon and moved to a spot near Laura and Ted. Raoul joined them. Peggy felt comfortable. *I could get used to this.*

After a moment, Peggy giggled. "I just thought of another verse." She stood up and cleared her throat.

People making cakes do it.
People jumping into lakes do it.
Some people don't even try to do it.

Xena ran to Peggy and they put their heads together.

Let's do it. Let's fall in love.

Then they took a bow.

TWELVE

Sunday, September 25

PEGGY READ A BOOK IN Raoul's living room. The party had ended late. It seemed to her that her life had become a constant party. Meanwhile she lived out of a suitcase and felt homeless.

Just as she was pondering this and life in general, Fran called to announce that she was going back to New Orleans.

"Why?" asked Peggy when Raoul told her about it.

"To help the Lambert family. It seems everyone is recovering from storm damage and Annie is by herself trying to clean up Agnes Lambert's house. Apparently there was flooding and many things are ruined. Fran has offered to go."

"Should we go and help her?" asked Peggy.

"I don't think it's necessary for you to go. But I said I would help since I'm now officially unemployed."

"You mean *self*-employed."

"Let's just say I'm available for travel," he said, sliding onto the sofa next to her.

"If you go, then I'm going," she said.

"You're busy at work. You have the new ocean temperature project to work on. You've been telling me how important it is."

"But Fran may have her hands full, especially if there's no one to help. I feel I should be there."

Raoul sighed. "I have a feeling I'm not going to win this one."

Peggy squeezed his arm. "You are a very perceptive man."

Monday, October 3

Peggy noticed a striking fact during her first day back in Agnes Lambert's neighborhood in Metairie, Louisiana: She didn't meet a single person who wasn't totally preoccupied with some aspect of storm recovery. It was all anyone talked about. It was all they did.

Along the streets Peggy saw great heaps of soggy wallboard and insulation, rolls of muddy carpet, mattresses splotched with mold, linens and pillows stained black, various furniture parts eaten away by rot and mold. In some spots the pile of residue was higher than the house from which it had been removed. Cars competed with trash for parking spaces.

The high water mark in a typical house was plainly visible on contents that were piled in front of it: an ever-present band of dirt around the bottoms of sofas, recliners, desks, bookcases, and appliances. Anything low to the ground was ruined. Pots and pans that had been in the lower levels of kitchen cabinets had become rusted scraps of metal. They were tossed onto the piles of trash along with toys, waterlogged stereos, swollen speakers, shoes, clothes, and books. The household debris was equally matched by tree trunks, branches, leaves and other natural storm residue.

"Who's going to pick this stuff up?" Peggy asked Annie as they returned to Agnes's house from a trip to a coffee shop.

"Jefferson Parish is supposed to be sending trucks around," said Annie. "Don't hold your breath." Then she paused. "On second thought, in some areas you must hold your breath."

"Have you noticed how similar all the piles of trash are?" asked Peggy. "When your belongings are in your house where they are supposed to be, you think of them as being unique and personal. But when everything is wet and moldy and sitting in a heap in your front yard, then it's just trash."

Annie looked at her. "I suppose it's comforting to know that your trash is just as trashy as your neighbor's."

Peggy laughed, then stopped herself. "Forgive me for seeing humor in this."

"We've got to laugh at something."

Peggy held styrofoam cups of iced coffee in her lap while Annie drove the car back to Agnes's house. It was a hot, bright afternoon. "So how have you been holding up?" she asked Annie, whose expression had a permanent look of tiredness.

"The kids finally went back to school today," Annie said. "That's a relief. But now they have this crazy schedule because their school is sharing classroom space with a high school that can't reopen. I don't know how those big high school kids fit in those little desks. But, whatever. My kids go in real early and come home early. Everything is chaotic. The mail still isn't being delivered. The phones don't work right; it takes twenty minutes of trying to get through to anybody."

Peggy was thinking of something to say when Annie said, "But you have to be careful who you complain to."

"Why?" asked Peggy.

"Because there's always somebody who's got it worse. Jeanette lived in Lakeview and lost everything. She's really feeling down."

"Where is she staying?"

"She's at my house with her kids. Her husband got reassigned to Baton Rouge and my husband's in Houston. It's a pain but we're happy they still have jobs."

"I believe you had a job as well, didn't you?" said Peggy.

"I was a dental hygienist, but there's absolutely no work. Nobody cares about their teeth at the moment. So I got laid off."

"Sorry to hear that. Did you get storm damage at your house?" asked Peggy.

Annie shook her head. "We live in River Ridge, which stayed dry."

They were stopped at an intersection and Peggy saw what was becoming a familiar sight: dozens of temporary signs advertising storm-related services. Katrina had become a cottage industry. If you needed mold treatment or carpet removed, or your roof repaired or a fallen tree chopped up, then all you had to do was drive to the nearest corner and write down some phone numbers. You could also buy new appliances, get your car repaired or hire a lawyer to sue the government.

When Peggy and Annie got back to the house with the iced coffee Raoul came out to greet them wearing the standard uniform of the day: yellow rubber gloves, face mask and white coverings over his shoes. The pile in front of the house had grown larger with the addition of a chair with a moldy seat cushion and a ruined television stand.

"We're making progress," he said.

She handed him an iced coffee. "I suppose we measure progress by the size of the trash pile," said Peggy.

Raoul paused and glanced up and down the street at the growing piles of debris. "As bad as this is, I'm told that it's nothing compared to what's within the city itself."

"That's exactly what Annie was just telling me."

Annie chimed in from behind them as she put her cell phone away. "As a matter of fact you'll get the grand tour. That was Jeanette. The city is saying they'll let Lakeview residents go in tomorrow. She would like us to come with her."

"I imagine there will be lots to clean," said Raoul.

Annie shielded her eyes from the glaring sun. "Actually, there won't be anything to clean. It's totaled. Hulie has had to go into the worst areas, since he's a contractor, and he said the neighborhoods that have been underwater for several weeks are like dead zones. He doesn't think there will be anything salvageable. I think Jeanette just wants company."

Peggy felt a certain weariness sink in as she ventured back into Agnes's house. She had been hoping the musty, moldy smell would magically go away, but it broke over her in waves as she stepped into the wrecked interior. The floors were bare concrete, the wood framing was exposed in the walls following the removal of the lower four feet of wallboard and insulation. The kitchen and bathroom cabinets were in the process of being carted out by Raoul. The smell of bleach mingled with mold. The refrigerator still worked, and everyone had heaped loads of praise on Peggy for having had the presence of mind to clean out the refrigerator and freezer when they evacuated before the storm.

Peggy donned her face mask and returned to her sorting task with Annie and Fran. It was one thing to go through storm-damaged property and sort good from bad, and fume over the indiscriminate nature of natural disasters. It was tragic, for example, that those awful coasters from Niagara Falls survived while your favorite recording of Pablo Casals didn't. But in the case of the Lambert family, the survivors also had to make decisions about passing on their departed mother's belongings. Agnes had not left detailed instructions in her will. It was up to the family members to agree on who got this or that item. One problem they faced is that the very people who wanted certain items were in no position to take them.

"Jeanette wants the old rocker," said Annie to her sister Shirley over the phone. "...I know she can't take it now, she wants someone to hold it... I don't have room and neither does Hulie... she can't afford to store it, and besides do you have any idea what it's like trying to get a storage unit around here? I called a few places and they laughed at me... Why don't you give her the dishes in exchange for the rocker? Talk to her, she needs dishes, she needs everything... Good luck...'Bye."

Peggy had suggested gathering like items together, thinking that it would make the choosing of keepsakes easier. Annie liked that idea, and within a few hours they had sorted several boxes of memorabilia. One was a box of Christian crosses collected during Agnes's travels to holy sites with her husband. Another box contained shot glasses and beer glasses, many from the same cities and towns as the crosses. One large box was filled with refrigerator magnets. "We're going to establish a rule for these magnets," Annie declared. "Whoever gave it to Mom gets it back."

Fran had compiled a box with nothing but menus and matchbooks from restaurants. "Look at this one," said

Fran. "It's from the Camellia Grill. Agnes and I used to go there when we were at Tulane together."

"I have a great story about the Camellia Grill," said Annie. "My Mom and Dad went there a lot when they were dating, and one of the guys behind the counter was a tall man who was bald on top and had black hair on the sides and black-rimmed glasses. He was a real character. Twenty-five years later when my husband and I were dating, we went to Camellia Grill all the time because we lived Uptown and that same man was still working there, still telling jokes and carrying on five conversations at once."

"What a timeless place," said Peggy.

Hulie arrived in his pickup truck late in the afternoon.

"What's all that junk in the back of your truck?" Annie asked when they had all gone outside for a break.

"You wouldn't believe what people are throwing away. That's a perfectly good refrigerator," said Hulie.

"But it probably had rotten food in it," said Annie.

"There was a couple of old cucumbers. I hosed it out and sprayed it with bleach. Good as new. You see, it's a Subzero, with the motor and all the electrical components mounted on top. Nothing critical got wet."

"That's disgusting."

"Check out this lawnmower. It started right up once I drained the water out of the crankcase. And look, somebody threw out these solid cypress beams because they were underwater," said Hulie, holding up some lengths of board.

"Do you think maybe they are moldy and rotten?" said Annie.

"This is cypress. It grows in water."

"Well, I say if you have space for all that junk, then maybe you should store some of Mom's stuff for Jeanette."

"I don't have space. I'm selling this stuff. I already have a buyer for the fridge, and I know somebody who can use the cypress."

Peggy considered this as she looked at the growing pile in front of Agnes's house. "Do you think we're throwing away salvageable items?" she asked.

Hulie shook his head as he surveyed the heap. "So far we haven't thrown away anything made of solid wood. Wood is more durable than people think. What is not durable is all this particle board crap. When it gets wet it expands like a sponge."

Peggy made a note to herself: Buy solid wood furniture if you live in a flood plain.

In the evening they gathered for dinner at Annie's house. "Chicken and rice is about all I can manage," she declared. It was generally noisy with everyone talking at once, but Jeanette was silent and brooding. Everyone knew what was on her mind. It was useless to try to talk about other things, because there was only one thing.

Tuesday, October 4

After the children had been deposited at their respective schools, Raoul loaded up Annie's car with boots, gloves and face masks. Hulie picked up Jeanette in his truck and the group made its away across Metairie toward the Orleans Parish line.

As they attempted to cross into the city limits they were stopped by a National Guardsman who explained that the mayor had announced earlier in the day that residents would not be allowed in.

Peggy could see Jeanette in front of them, leaning over Hulie to talk to the guard.

"She must be furious," Annie said.

Finally Hulie made a U-turn and Annie followed. Then Hulie turned down another street and drove through a rundown neighborhood with the now-familiar trash piles out front.

"This is known as Bucktown," said Annie. "Hulie's going to try to drive over the 17th Street Canal."

When they reached the Bucktown bridge that crossed the canal, a military guard waved them through without stopping.

"Isn't that typical?" said Annie. "Nobody's in charge around here."

Peggy tried to get her bearings. "Wait, did you say 17th Street Canal? Isn't that the one that failed and caused the flooding?"

"You got it," said Annie. "One of several, actually." She slowed the car and pointed. "I think the breach was right where those cranes are working."

"Do they know yet what caused the failure?" asked Peggy.

"If you want my opinion, somebody knows but they aren't telling."

Peggy was not prepared for the sight that greeted her when they crossed the canal into Lakeview. If Metairie and Kenner had seemed like the edge of a war zone, this was ground zero.

The streets and sidewalks were covered with dried, cracked mud. There was not a blade of grass in sight. The entire place had one color: brown. It looked to Peggy like someone had drained a lake and uncovered an ancient civilization.

The houses were muddy up to a point just above the doorway. Peggy was shocked to realize what this meant: The water had risen to the ceilings.

House after house, submerged. Lawns and gardens, dead.

They rode in silence, too stunned to speak. The streets were empty except for one or two recovery crews. No one paid any attention to them as they slowly rounded a corner and headed toward Jeanette's house.

Peggy had the sensation that they should not be there. City officials were right to keep people out, she thought. It was not inhabitable.

Jeanette's house was like the others. Orange hieroglyphics were spray-painted above the front door, above which a dirty line indicated the high water mark.

With an air of resignation, Jeanette donned her yellow gloves and approached the house. She peeked through a broken window, then pushed hard on the door to get it to budge. She stepped into the place that had been her home.

As Peggy followed the others, she felt something squishy beneath her boots. She was sickened to realize that, under the dead leaves and tree branches, the yard was coated with a thick layer of black sludge. She tried not to think of exactly what it contained, but she knew it was indistinguishable from sewage.

The moment she looked inside the front door, Peggy realized that she had no idea what a house looked like after it had been submerged in water. She could see that the contents had floated, and then simply fallen into a pile in the middle of the room when the water drained out. All the furniture was turned over and covered with mud: a television, a futon, a cabinet with doors, a wet pile of blankets and pillows. On top of the television rested a few pots and pans from the kitchen.

Annie pointed to a ceiling light fixture caked with mud. "That used to be white."

In the kitchen, the refrigerator rested sideways on the table. The sink and countertops were layered with slime. Two inches of mud covered the floor. The fumes from sewage and rot made the air unhealthy to breathe.

Peggy heard Jeanette cry out from a back room. The attic door was hanging open and she had spotted a couple of boxes that appeared to be okay. Raoul fetched them from the attic and handed them to Peggy, who stood on an overturned dresser because there was not an inch of floor space that was clear. Later, when they were all outside, Jeanette removed her gloves and opened a box. It contained Christmas decorations. She laughed and cried at the same time. "My husband never liked these ornaments, but I loved them because they were so corny, so typical of New Orleans."

Peggy walked around the house into the backyard. On the back porch, dried, cracked mud baked in the sun. Two giant trees were uprooted. A garden that she guessed once contained lush greenery was now dead and brown.

In the end, Jeanette had no interest in removing anything else from the house. "As far as I'm concerned they can bulldoze it," she said, holding the box of ornaments tightly. Peggy detected not sadness, but relief. Jeanette no longer had to wonder about her house. She knew. It was gone. A phase of her life, one that included having a mother and a house, had come to an abrupt end.

They got into their cars and drove away. They had seen enough. Peggy felt a headache and a bout of depression seeping into her consciousness. She drank water and couldn't escape the smell of sewage lingering in her clothes and hair. She considered throwing the clothes away instead of packing them in her suitcase.

As they drove out of the flood zone it occurred to Peggy that she was seeing the land in its natural state. It was probably always a flood plain, she thought, a place where water naturally collected when nearby Lake Ponchartrain overflowed its banks, which probably happened many times over thousands of years. But then someone figured out a way to fill in the flood plain and build houses on it. As they drove out of Lakeview she noticed, remarkably, that many of the homes were built flat on the ground. Others, of course, were built high, as she expected. But many weren't and she wondered why builders were ever allowed to build unraised houses in a flood plain.

She turned to Raoul. "You know, we've gone full circle."

"What do you mean?"

"It all started with a flood, at Fran's house in Westport. And now we're right back in a flood zone where people were allowed to build houses in places where perhaps there shouldn't be a house."

"And are we going to rehash all that we've argued about since then?"

Peggy fumed as she stared at the destruction. It always came back to money, she realized. Developers will build houses as long as there are people willing to buy them. It's almost an act of political suicide to get in the middle of those transactions and say, 'Sorry, you can't build houses there.'

On the way back to Annie's, Hulie led them on a detour to a farm stand in St. Rose, down River Road, west of New Orleans.

"I heard he had opened back up," said Hulie, purchasing a basket of large Creole tomatoes. "We need a return to normal around here."

Peggy stood with Fran and looked at the long green levee that ran between River Road and the Mississippi River. A fresh breeze touched their faces.

"There. Feel that?" said Fran. "That balmy breeze. That smell of flowers and moisture. That's the Louisiana I remember. It's still here."

Peggy smelled it, too. But to her it seemed fragile, like the dunes and grasses along the Pacific Coast. It was something that should be protected from development.

Peggy and Raoul boarded a plane that evening. She felt her strength drained from her as she contemplated the work that lay ahead for the Lambert family. It's like starting completely over, she realized. They traveled in silence. Eventually Peggy rested her head on Raoul's shoulder and closed her eyes.

THIRTEEN

Monday, October 10

"WHAT WERE THEY THINKING?" KELLY fumed on the morning ferry. He and Paula sat across from Peggy. Paula studied a thread that appeared to be out of place on her skirt.

"Who committed a blunder this time, Kel?" Peggy asked.

"The entire U.S. House of Representatives," Kelly said as he turned the pages of his newspaper. "I blame all of them for not getting their collective heads out of their arses."

Peggy paused. "I can think of a couple of events recently that fit that description. Which one has got your attention?"

"Just last week, the House approved a bill, by two votes, that would make it easier for oil companies to build new refineries."

"Ah, that's a good one," said Peggy.

"There won't be as much environmental oversight, they will be allowed to eliminate some grades of gasoline, they can use federal lands, such as closed military installations, without local consent. The list goes on. Who in their right mind would vote for new refineries when there won't be anything for them to refine in a few years?"

"They had to do some serious arm twisting just to get the two-vote margin," said Peggy. "That shows you how bad it was."

Paula had a stern expression as she said, "Some people simply aren't capable of seeing past next week. That's why they support idiotic projects like that."

"And would one of those people be…"

"Luke? You guessed it." She shook her head with exasperation. "I took him to see a film called the *End of Suburbia*, which tells the story of the growth of suburbs and how that whole way of life is totally dependent on cheap energy. To me, and to anyone with half a brain, it's obvious that we need to get off fossil fuels. Well, he must not meet the half-a-brain criteria because the first thing he starts talking about afterwards is how somebody has to do something about the price of gas." She slapped her high forehead. "Luke, wake up. There's not going to be any cheap gas. Those days are over. And then I told him my pet theory, that gasoline should really be, like, five dollars a gallon."

"Fine by me," said Kelly.

"He thought I lost my marbles," said Paula.

Peggy laughed.

Paula looked dejected. "We ended up having a big argument and, well, I must have scared him off or something because the very next evening he cancelled a date we had made. And guess where he went instead?"

"Back to Florence," said Peggy.

Paula's face looked like someone had carved it out of granite. "That woman must have some kind of radar that goes off whenever a man is even remotely available," she said.

This was a new side of her, Peggy realized. Paula had seemed a quiet and mild-mannered young lady who sewed herself a new skirt every weekend, but now she was on fire. It showed that you don't really know people until something happens that sets them off.

"You've just reminded me of something I've had on my mind," said Peggy. "Not Luke, I mean, but the part about suburbs."

Both Paula and Kelly stopped what they were doing. She chose her words carefully because the concept was only half-formed in her mind.

"I was reading an article in yesterday's *New York Times* about the pumps that are used to keep floodwaters out of New Orleans. At one time it was a world-class system of pumps and levees, but today they are still using pumps that were built in 1913. Oh, and by the way, some of the old pumps worked better than the new ones. So much for our engineering prowess. The real message in the article was how we are not investing in our infrastructure the way we once did."

"You can see that in the kinds of things cities spend money on these days," said Kelly.

"Exactly. Communities seem more likely to invest in new retail development projects or housing than infrastructure," said Peggy.

"Infrastructure isn't sexy," said Paula.

"And it doesn't generate revenue," said Kelly.

"You've hit the nail on the head. It's all about revenue. It's all about bringing money in the door right now instead of investing in something with long-term benefits. Roads and schools and public transportation and alternative energy projects all take a long time to pay off."

Peggy took a sip of her tea and saw a faint orange glow appear beyond the city.

"Do you have a plan for fixing that?" asked Kelly.

"It's just a concept, an idea. I have this crazy notion of trying to change the status quo. How do we get communities to value infrastructure as much as they value stores and condos? I don't know how. I'm hoping Raoul will help me."

"Have you told him about it?" said Paula.

"Not really," said Peggy. "He was greatly affected by what we saw in New Orleans. His reaction has been to withdraw and play music and work in his garden. He's not the change-the-world type. He has a theory that people have a midlife crisis every year after they turn fifty, and they dream of leaving their mark on the world."

Paula frowned. "That's kind of gloomy."

"I hope he's wrong." This was one of those moments when Peggy missed Taylor. He would have encouraged her. Even if the task were hopeless, he would urge her to try. She felt a measure of strength from thinking of him. She wanted to feel that same strength from Raoul.

Tuesday, October 11

The conversation started at the kitchen counter, where Raoul was tossing roasted vegetables and pasta with oil and capers and fresh herbs. Peggy had come over for dinner. Since the latest New Orleans trip, she had been staying at her own house. She was simply too busy to deal with the extra commuting and having to live out of a suitcase.

"Smell that?" he said, waving the aromatic steam toward his face.

"I'm thinking of starting a club," Peggy blurted out.

"What are clubs? Do you have them with pasta?"

"No. I'm talking about an organization of people dedicated to a common purpose."

Raoul shook with laughter. "My mind was on food. I was trying to think of a food item called a club."

"Or should it be a newsletter? Maybe a club and a newsletter."

"What are you talking about?"

"I'm getting ahead of myself."

"You're already miles ahead of me, but I'm getting used to that."

She tried to compose her thoughts as they sat down to eat. "I'm becoming very annoyed with the way things are going in our society."

"Join the club. Um, sorry, I wasn't trying to be funny."

"I know. But starting a club is a way of finding like-minded people who want to change the status quo."

"Agreed. You could convene a weekly breakfast group and discuss the issues of the day."

She gave him a stern look. "That's not what I had in mind. I don't want to chat about the ruination of society over blueberry muffins at the diner. I want action."

Raoul paused with a fork in the air. "I get it," he said quietly. "You want to make a difference."

"Yes."

"You're tired of the way things are, and you want to change them."

"Yes."

"Starting with, for example, elevated highways along the Seattle waterfront."

She thought for a moment. "I suppose that's a fair example of a bad infrastructure decision that could be remedied."

"Good. In my opinion, that noisy, smelly monstrosity is the biggest wart in all of Seattle, and I can't believe people are quibbling over the few pennies per gallon of gas that it would take to build a tunnel and tear down the highway."

She banged the table with her fist. "Now you're talking. That's exactly what I've been saying. No one wants to think about investing for the long term. Imagine the waterfront without that raised highway. It would be wonderful."

"Every square foot of waterfront property would triple in value overnight." Then Raoul's eyes widened. "Maybe we should buy a condo before they build the tunnel."

Peggy at first started to object on conflict-of-interest grounds. But then one word in his sentence stood out. "We?" she said.

"Just a figure of speech. Can I get you more water?" He got up quickly to fill the water glasses, which didn't need refilling.

However, Peggy was not one to let words fall on the floor without notice. She decided to file that one away for further consideration.

"Okay," said Peggy. "I think you have the idea. Does that mean you're willing to help me organize my club? Or would you rather edit the newsletter?"

"Your club has one member and you're already launching a newsletter?"

"No. My club has two members."

He looked at her. "I see. I imagine the two members are at this table."

She reached over the table and placed her hand on his arm. "I need your help."

"You appear to be serious about this."

"Very."

"In that case, you can count on me for legal advice."

"Thank you, but I want more than that. I need your involvement. You're a great organizer. You can help me get this thing off the ground."

"You need a mission statement."

"See what I mean! You think in terms of mission statements."

"But you're overlooking one thing: I'm not the activist type."

"It's never too late to start."

"I don't wish to start. I like not being an activist. I get to spend my evenings at home playing music and planning next year's potato garden. Kelly's really got me hooked on this potato thing."

"But how does that accomplish anything?" Peggy complained.

"It accomplishes the playing of music and the growing of potatoes. Do you think I have room for two long rows?"

"Don't ignore me, like I'm a child."

"I would never do that."

"Then why aren't you taking me seriously?"

"Because you don't realize what you're up against."

"You forget that citizens have the power to change things."

"True, but you need a lot of citizens who don't mind paying more for gas in order to replace an ugly highway with a tunnel. What you are talking about comes down to expensive long-term projects that are publicly funded and which do not, in general, get politicians reelected."

"We have to change hearts and minds," she said.

"Now you're talking like a crusader. I'm not a crusader," he explained. "I've outgrown those tendencies. Which reminds me, don't you have a birthday coming up?"

"I knew you were going to say that." She leaned forward, and felt anger rising within her. "Don't even think about giving me your midlife crisis lecture."

"Trust me, I wasn't going to do any such thing, especially when you're holding a knife and fork."

"You're making fun of me, aren't you? You know, you talk a good line, but deep down I think you're self-centered and insecure."

He thought for a moment. "I love the saying, 'All politics is local.' To me it means very local, like 'it's all about me.'"

"That's a very selfish outlook," she said.

"But it's an honest outlook. It's what's at the heart of rational economic behavior. People are supposed to look out for their own best interests. If everybody truly did that, we would be pretty well off. The real problem is that people jump on bandwagons and get wound up over dubious causes just because they like having something to whine about." He resumed eating. "Sorry. I'm not an activist and I don't plan to become one."

"I don't think you get it. If building houses on flood plains is your idea of rational economic behavior, then I would say your notion of rational is pretty irrational. I think *myopic* is the word I'm looking for."

"It's not for us to assume that everyone thinks long-term."

"Well, maybe we can get them to think that way."

"We're right back to your club, aren't we?"

She slumped in her chair. She hadn't intended to get into a fight with Raoul. She had to treat him as merely the first naysayer, the first person she must convert to her cause.

After all, if she couldn't talk one self-centered, property rights advocate into it, then how could she hope to change millions of hearts and minds?

They switched topics and finished the meal amiably, but Peggy was troubled by not getting the kind of support she wanted from Raoul.

FOURTEEN

Friday, October 14

PEGGY TOOK THE EARLY FERRY into town, feeling exhausted. She had been on an erratic schedule the entire week, collecting research results from three different ocean monitoring teams that were involved in a detailed study of water temperatures. There were deadlines, and Milton was as excited and impatient as a child. She'd spent hours on the phone with people in far-off time zones. But it was okay, it took her mind off everything else.

As she made her way to her usual seat she saw that her regular commuting buddies were all there.

"Look what the cat dragged in," said Florence, sitting next to Luke, who looked dapper and cheerful.

"Morning, Peggy," said Kelly.

Luke waved. Paula, sitting across from Luke, moved over to make room for Peggy. "Good morning," Paula said.

"Hello to everyone." Peggy was certain they were all thinking that she had been sequestered away in a little love nest with Raoul all week, staring dreamily into his eyes by a crackling fire. I've been working! she wanted to say emphatically.

The truth was that she had not spoken to Raoul since her failed bid to get him to support the club she wanted to organize. She was a bit piqued over that, but decided to leave him alone and let him come around at his own pace. Besides, she had her own work.

"How's Raoul these days?" asked Florence, not wasting a moment. Her legs were crossed, allowing one bare knee to peek out from beneath her long raincoat. Luke could not seem to take his eyes off of it.

"Raoul is probably bored out of his mind," said Peggy.

"Poor thing," said Florence. "He must be pining away for, um, someone."

"Surely he's doing something," said Kelly. "The man has more hobbies than one person should be allowed."

"He has too many hobbies. They're all about him, if you get right down to it," said Peggy.

"Ooh, I'm so glad you joined us today, Peggy," said Florence, her face lighting up. "We want to hear all about it."

Peggy had always been astonished at Florence's appetite for bad news about other people's relationships. She wondered if Luke knew that Florence would drop him like last week's hair color if Raoul were suddenly "on the market."

"There's nothing to tell," said Peggy. "I've been working like a maniac all week and I have not even spoken to Raoul since last weekend. I was only joking when I said he was bored. For all I know he's having a ball."

"I left two messages and he hasn't returned them," said Kelly.

"Really?" said Peggy.

Kelly looked embarrassed. "I lost Xena's phone number, and so I called Raoul to ask for it."

"I called as well," said Paula. "When I didn't see you on the ferry this week I called your house, and when you didn't answer I called Raoul's."

"And there was no answer?" asked Peggy. All thoughts of Florence flew from her mind. Peggy looked at her watch. Almost six. "Excuse me. He'll probably hate me for this but I've got to know if he's okay." She removed her cell phone from her purse and walked down the passageway. His phone rang and rang, then his voice mail answered. Peggy left a brief message.

She returned to her seat, very silent. The others chatted about the local news of the day. Peggy listened but her thoughts kept straying to Raoul. Was he okay?

The ferry docked on schedule. Peggy collected her things and followed Paula across the pedestrian ramp to the terminal. She walked in silence. Thinking. At the end of the terminal, at the point where she would ordinarily continue over the footbridge that led to First Avenue, she stopped.

Paula must have sensed it, because she stopped, too. "Are you okay?"

"Not really. I feel silly, but I'm worried about Raoul. We had an argument the other night and I haven't spoken with him, and now he's not answering his phone at six o'clock in the morning."

"Hmm. That is worrisome," said Paula.

Peggy took a deep breath. "I'm getting right back on that boat."

Paula's eyes widened. "Are you sure?"

"Yes. I've got to check on him. My stomach is tied up in knots. If I don't go, I'll spend all day being sick about it."

"Do you want me to come with you?"

"Thanks. But I'll manage."

Paula hugged Peggy. "Good luck. Call me when you hear something."

They parted, and Peggy got back on the ferry to return to the island. She fidgeted in her seat the entire way, and when the boat finally docked, Peggy rushed down the ramp, leaving in her wake a trail of curious morning commuters. She quickly walked the distance to her house and got directly into her car. She thought about going in first to check for messages but decided there wasn't time.

It normally took Peggy about ten minutes to drive to Rolling Bay. She made it in eight.

There was no answer when she knocked on Raoul's door. She used her own key, and was reminded of how familiar it was to let herself into Raoul's house, and how, for the past week, she had been away from that routine, and missed it.

"Raoul," she called out as she entered. "Raoul, are you here?"

Something about the quiet echo that reached her ears told her the house was empty. The gray morning light coming through the windows made everything look ghostly. She switched on a light, which brightened the room, but did not warm it.

She shivered and walked slowly toward the bedroom. "Raoul?"

Raoul's bed was made. She sat on it and smoothed the comforter with her hand. It was cool. She didn't think the bed had been slept in recently.

Peggy searched the entire house and the garage. His motorcycle was gone, along with his helmet, boots and riding clothes. She returned to the bedroom and walked through it to the bathroom. His toothbrush was gone. But she noticed on the counter an almost-empty tube of toothpaste, flattened into a curved, bumpy spine. She checked the bathroom closet. A new tube of toothpaste that had been on the shelf was gone.

She opened his bedroom closet and tried to figure out what was missing. The suits he wore most often hung neatly from the bar. His dress shoes rested side by side on the floor. Therefore he didn't go on a business trip, she thought, or at least he didn't dress for one. She pulled open a dresser drawer, but she couldn't figure out what, if anything, was missing.

In the kitchen, by the door leading to the garage, she looked carefully at the pile of shoes. Her own garden clogs were among them, looking right at home. Raoul's sandals rested one on top the other. What was missing? Then it hit her: an old pair of running shoes was gone. That gave her an idea. She crossed the room to a hall closet and rummaged through it. Raoul kept a backpack there that he used when he rode his motorcycle. It was gone.

Peggy put on a kettle of water for tea. Her hands trembled as she reached for the dial to turn on the flame. It came alive, the first sign of life she had witnessed since entering the house. She collected her thoughts: Raoul went on a motorcycle trip and took his backpack and running shoes and a toothbrush with a new tube of toothpaste.

Then Peggy snapped her fingers; maybe he wrote something down! She looked on the kitchen counter near the phone and found only a few old scraps of paper with phone numbers scrawled on them. Nothing new. On his desk she searched for a business card or a brochure that looked like it might be recent, or might provide a reason for a sudden trip without telling your… Peggy paused. What was she, exactly? Friend? Girlfriend? What was her status? She felt annoyed suddenly that she didn't have a clearly defined status with Raoul.

The phone rang. Peggy literally jumped into the air. She calmed herself with a few seconds of controlled breathing, and then answered.

"Hello, who's this?" said a woman's voice. Peggy recognized the voice of Deidre.

"Deidre, it's me, Peggy."

"Oh, thank God someone's home," said Deidre. "I've been trying to call Dad for a couple of days. Did you two go on a trip or something?"

Peggy was stunned. This was more serious than she had realized. "Deidre, I have not been with your father. I've been at home all week, working, but then I got worried when he didn't return my calls. So I came to his house this morning. He seems to have gone off on a trip."

"Alone?"

"Well, uh..." She had not considered that possibility. She cleared her throat. "Here are the facts: his motorcycle is gone, and he took a backpack with his running shoes, toothbrush and toothpaste."

"That's it?"

"I imagine he took some clothes. I've only figured out that much."

"He didn't call you before he left?" Deidre's voice had an edge.

"No." Peggy could not rid her mind of a nagging thought: What if Raoul had gone away to meet someone, a secret lover, a romantic rendezvous in the country? Would he take his motorcycle? Maybe she also rode a motorcycle. He would dress casually, and bring only a toothbrush and toothpaste. She would be in a leather motorcycle suit, and underwear. After all, one doesn't need much for those kinds of trips. This was a ridiculous line of reasoning, Peggy told herself.

"It's not like him at all," Deidre said. "Are you sure there are no notes lying around?"

"I checked everywhere. I was hoping to find a phone number, or something that might indicate where he has gone."

As she held the cordless phone to her ear, Peggy went back to the desk and looked again. Perhaps there was something she had overlooked, perhaps a brochure advertising cabins in the mountains, small cozy cabins with nothing but a wood stove and a giant bearskin rug. She imagined him there with only his running shoes and a toothbrush. And a motorcycle babe.

"This is not like Dad at all," said Deidre.

"You can say that again."

A shrill whistle from the kitchen interrupted Peggy's thoughts.

"What's that?" asked Deidre.

"The kettle. I'm going to drink some tea and think this through. Then I'm going to go home and check my e-mails and phone messages. Perhaps he sent me something that I overlooked."

"Please call me the minute you know something," pleaded Deidre.

"Of course. And by the way, how's Taylor? He never calls me anymore."

"I guess I'm a distraction," she said. "He's coming this weekend. I'll sit him down and make him call."

"Thanks. Take care, Deidre. I love you." Peggy hung up. She didn't know why she said that. She had never spoken that way to Deidre before.

She sat on the sofa and drank her tea. But she couldn't relax. She stared into empty space with her hands on her tea mug and her feet and knees held tightly together. After a while she felt a strong urge to return to her house and check for messages. There might be a brief message waiting at this very moment, she thought. Or, better yet, an invitation. "Join me in the mountains. When can you get here? It's lovely. Pack as little as possible."

Then Peggy realized that she should also call her boss. She finished her tea quickly and left Raoul's.

Peggy drove back to her house in a hurry. She was operating on nervous energy. A tired feeling crept over her, and the day had barely started. She screeched to a halt in her driveway and then, in her rush to get from the car to the house, she did the one thing she absolutely did not want to do at that moment: She locked her keys in her car. She realized it the instant she slammed the car door shut, just after mashing down the little button that locks all the doors.

Standing in front of the door to her house, she felt energy drain from her. Inside her house she was sure there were messages, perhaps numerous messages, from Raoul. She did her controlled breathing exercises. They always helped during moments of stress. It reminded her of being in labor. In those days no one taught you how to breathe during labor, but she had a midwife who was skilled in many practical aspects of child birthing. "Your body will forget to breathe," she had said. "Your brain must order the body to breathe. Decide to breathe. Slowly...there! Don't be in a hurry to exhale." Peggy remembered those words and the sound of the midwife's voice almost thirty years later as she stood on her front stoop, locked out of her house and car.

A happy thought came to her. She had her purse! It was attached to her shoulder like an extension of her body. She must have grabbed it without thinking. She snatched her cell phone from the bag and held it like gold. Then she called her boss.

"You did what?!" said Milton.

Peggy cringed. Milton was a slave to deadlines and Peggy knew she would miss hers.

"I locked myself out of my house and car," Peggy repeated.

"But how can that be an issue when you're in Seattle? Just walk to the office and we'll straighten it out before you go home today."

"I'm on Bainbridge Island." She then told the story of how she had unexpectedly returned to the island to check on Raoul.

"Oh," was all he said. But it was enough. He was clearly not happy.

"Look, Milton. I'm sorry, but that's the state of things. Now if you'll excuse me I'll see if I can get into my house and get my spare car key, or else I'll walk down to the police station and ask them to break into my car. They know how to do those things, I believe."

"Right, they'll do it," he said without a trace of enthusiasm. "Let me know how it goes, okay?"

Peggy hung up and began to think through her options. She had not given a house key to any of her neighbors; in fact, she hadn't really made friends with her neighbors. It was not like her former life in Ballard, where she and Taylor had many friends. Good friends, lifelong friends, people who knew every detail of your life, like what kind of cereal your kids ate for breakfast and what music you listened to and what books you read and how often you cleaned your kitchen. She had no one like that in her new neighborhood.

Peggy turned away from her house and walked to the police station near the ferry terminal. A policewoman named Mandy agreed to come and unlock Peggy's car. Several minutes later, Peggy stood in her driveway and watched Mandy pedal up the hill on her police mountain bike. She wore shorts in spite of the brisk air.

With quiet efficiency, Mandy unlocked the door with a long, flat strip of metal that she slid between the door and window.

"Wow," said Peggy. "That was too easy."

"With older cars especially," Mandy said. "Is there anything else I can help you with?"

Peggy paused as a thought came to her. "Maybe. How does one go about reporting a missing person?"

Mandy's eyes widened. "That's a bit more serious than locking your keys in your car."

"It's probably nothing. The fact is, I have a friend I haven't heard from and I just went to his house and he wasn't there and it appears he's gone off on his motorcycle. But the unusual thing is that he didn't tell anyone where he was going."

Mandy straddled her bicycle and donned her helmet. "So you don't know if he's in trouble or if he has just chosen to be alone."

Peggy gasped. "What kind of trouble?"

Mandy shrugged. "Is he wealthy? Or ill? If he's wealthy he could have been abducted, if he's ill he could have just wandered off without knowing what he was doing."

"He's not that wealthy and he's not ill," said Peggy. "He went off on his motorcycle and packed very little."

"How do you know what he took with him?"

Peggy blushed a bit. "I'm sort of a regular guest at his house."

"I see," said Mandy, doing a poor job of hiding the amusement in her voice.

Peggy squirmed and turned two shades of red.

"Have you searched the entire house?" asked Mandy. "Do you really know everything that he took with him? The reason I'm saying that is because my boyfriend rides a motorcycle and it's amazing how much stuff you can carry on those things if you really wanted to. He goes camping and fishing on his bike."

"Camping?" Peggy said. A new thought came to her. "Excuse me. I need to make some calls. You just gave me an idea."

Mandy turned her bicycle around. "Why don't you at least give me your phone number and if somebody reports a man in trouble I'll contact you."

"Okay. Thanks." Peggy scribbled her cell phone number on the back of her business card and handed it to the policewoman.

Peggy raced into her house with her newly-retrieved keys. There were no voice mail messages from Raoul. Peggy turned on her computer and listened to the whine of the fan and the buzzing of the hard drive and watched the meaningless display of symbols and logos parade across her screen like credits for a bad movie. When it was ready, she went straight to her mail and reviewed recent messages: several work-related notes, one from Marjorie, one from an old friend in Ballard. Nothing from Raoul.

Then she dialed Deidre's number. Deidre answered at once.

"Does your father have any camping equipment?" Peggy asked.

"Yes, on the metal shelves in the garage. Why? What have you learned?"

"Nothing yet, but I realized that I could be overlooking an important clue. After all I'm not as familiar with your father's possessions as some people think."

"What's that supposed to mean?"

Peggy relayed the story of the policewoman.

"You went to the police?"

"I locked my keys in the car and I had to ask them to break in for me."

"You're having quite a morning, aren't you?"

Peggy sighed. "I feel like a strange day is just beginning. I'm going back to Raoul's to check the garage. If he took the camping stuff, where would he have gone?"

"It depends on what he took. Call me when you get there and I'll tell you exactly what to look for."

Twelve minutes later Peggy stood in Raoul's garage with her cell phone to her ear. Deidre was on the other end.

"Look at the high shelf next to the wall, all the way to the right. See it?"

"Yes."

"Second shelf from the top there should be a small gray nylon bag. It holds a small camping tent."

"I don't see it," said Peggy excitedly.

"Look around the floor. Look on the other shelves."

"I'm looking. I'm looking. I don't see the gray bag." It was a fairly neat place, as garages go. Peggy scanned the contents of the shelves and saw tools, coolers, gardening equipment, paints, oils, but nothing that looked like a small tent in a gray bag.

"Now look for a red backpack," said Deidre.

"I definitely do not see a red backpack. I'm looking everywhere."

"That contains his camping overalls and a couple of flannel shirts."

"Ah. So he's not frolicking about in just his running shoes."

"That doesn't sound like Dad."

"That's just me. I tend to imagine the worst possible scenarios. Okay, so far he has a tent and the red backpack. What else?"

"Sleeping bag."

Peggy again followed instructions but could not locate a blue lightweight sleeping bag that should have been next to the gray tent bag.

There was excitement in Deidre's voice. "It means he's camping somewhere very close. Right on the island. There aren't many spots: Fort Ward, Fay Bainbridge. Oh, but wait, there's also Blake Island. Dad and Mom used to borrow a boat and go camping on Blake Island."

"What would he do with the motorcycle?"

Deidre paused. "I believe their friend, Mr. Ed, had a boathouse or something. Dad could have parked his bike in it and taken the motorboat."

"Why wouldn't he have driven his car?"

"It's hard to say. It's worth checking on, though."

"Do you have their number?"

"It's in Mom's address book, which is on Dad's desk."

Peggy walked back into the house with the phone still to her ear. "What's the name?"

"Sorry, I only knew him as Mr. Ed. I don't remember their last name. But look for an Ed and Jenny in Eagledale."

It was a big book with lots of pages covered with writing from many different pens and pencils. "This will take time," said Peggy. "I think I'll try the local camping places first: Fort Ward and Fay Bainbridge. Any others?"

"I'm sure there are others, such as private lands."

"Okay. Gotta run. I'll stay in touch. Love you." Peggy hung up and fished around for a good map of Bainbridge Island.

She went out to her car and squinted; the sun was high and bright by this time. She unfolded the map on the seat next to her and at last felt like she had something to do besides worry. She had a goal. She was looking for a man on a motorcycle with a red backpack and a blue sleeping bag. That shouldn't be too hard: Bainbridge was a small island.

She left the Rolling Bay area in a hurry, at one point spinning her tires on a bit of gravel in the road as she turned north toward Fay Bainbridge State Park. The tall, graceful evergreens swept past her window unnoticed, as did the colorful clusters of maple and birch trees. There was a fresh fall dampness in the air, in addition to the strong sunlight. But she hardly noticed any of this because her mind was on Raoul; specifically, on how little she really knew about him.

She felt she had gotten to know the present-day Raoul: his tastes, his hobbies, his conversational style. She had met his friends. She loved talking to him and, although she found him interesting, she had to admit there was a streak of the ordinary about him. He was...predictable. An old memory struck her: Taylor had been the same way. In fact, her mother had used those same words: "Taylor is a safe, predictable man," she had said, and then she added "...just right for you, I think." Peggy remembered not liking that part. She was in her late twenties at the time and it was somehow not very flattering to be judged a good mate for a safe, predictable man.

Yet Peggy knew there was more to a person, especially a sixtyish person, than what he or she is like in the present day. She knew that Raoul had probably lived through many phases of life. He might have had a wild twentyish phase, and a fatherly fortyish phase, and he might be unrecognizable to Peggy if she could go back in time and secretly observe him. We were all somebody else at one time or another, she told herself.

Priscilla. That was one part of Raoul's life that Peggy did not know much about. She had to admit that Raoul didn't know much about Taylor either. They were each keenly aware of the other's late spouse, aware that an entire life was lived before they had met. In fact, it was probably the most important thing they had in common. They each recognized when to provide comfort, and when to provide solitude. A part of each of them lived in this great, dark, unfathomable space called grief.

As she drew closer to the campground, Peggy thought to herself that she already knew it would be a dead end. She felt his absence as she drove into the park and steered down the narrow lane that descended to the beach and emerged onto a parking lot. It was deserted. She drove along the empty campsites and parked at the far end, then walked over the jumble of driftwood logs to the rocky shore. The wind filled her jacket and vest with air and puffed it up like a marshmallow. She felt moisture and could see the mists piling up over Puget Sound.

For several minutes she tried to imagine where Raoul would pitch his tent and enjoy a few days of solitude. Surely Priscilla was part of this. He missed Priscilla and was with her in spirit. It was not solitude. He had the company of his memories. She hurried back to the car. It had to be Blake Island. She decided she wouldn't even bother checking Fort Ward, the other camping site Deidre had mentioned.

When Peggy got back to the car her cell phone rang.

"Well?" said Milton.

"I haven't found Raoul."

"But did you get into your car?"

"Yes. I'm going to Blake Island."

"Blake Island? What for?"

"I think Raoul went there," she said while starting her car and driving out of the park. Somehow just saying it made her more convinced it was true.

"What on earth would he go there for?"

"Camping."

"Camping?"

"Yes, camping."

"With whom?"

Peggy almost answered "his late wife" but decided that would simply invite more questions than she had time to answer. "I think he wants to be alone," she said.

Milton was silent; Peggy imagined him processing things as she sped south back to Raoul's house. She was going to get the address book and hunt down Ed and Jenny in Eagledale.

"The reason I called," said Milton, "is to tell you that an unexpected opportunity has fallen into our laps."

"Oh, and what would that be?"

"The head of one of the leading ocean preservation societies is in town and wants to meet us for dinner."

Peggy knew what was coming and began to prepare an excuse. "By any chance do you mean Dr. Hanford Hinckley, the famous oceanographer from Woods Hole, Massachusetts?"

"Exactly. He wants to talk about the grant we applied for."

Peggy had always admired Milton for being so tenacious when it came to finding money for the organization. Without his efforts she would not have had a job all these years. "He's way over my head," said Peggy.

"You'd better have somebody like Dr. Forest. He's a scientist."

"But Dr. Hinckley is impressed with our latest ocean project and wants to hear more about it, and you're the one who has the best grasp of the data."

Peggy pulled over to the side of the road. "Milton. I'm very sorry. I'm in the middle of a personal crisis and I can't go out to dinner and carry on an engaging conversation with a brilliant scientist. I don't care how wealthy his foundation is."

Again he was silent. Then Milton spoke very carefully. "I would like you to make sure you've thought this through. You're going to miss a potentially career-enhancing conversation in order to find someone who perhaps doesn't want to be found."

Peggy stared through the window of her car. What if he's right? What if Raoul doesn't want to be found?

"On the other hand," she said, "what if he's injured, or stranded and can't contact anyone? I have to know, even if it means I've intruded on his seclusion."

"So you're doing this for you?"

"Milton, let's just say I think I know what I'm doing and leave it at that, shall we? Now if you will send my regrets to Dr. Hinckley I will be off to lovely Blake Island."

Milton grumbled something that she did not quite catch as she stepped on the gas and sent a spray of gravel into the shrubbery on the side of the road. Her hand trembled as she dropped the phone into her purse. She had never dismissed her boss before. It felt exhilarating.

The name was Semp. Ed and Jenny Semp. Peggy figured it out by accident. After an initial slow drive through the few streets that make up the sparse community known as Eagledale, Peggy pulled over to study the map and

Raoul's address book. As she took a sip from her water bottle she realized it had gone stale: the bottle had been in the car for several days. She got out of her car to stretch her legs and pour out the water. From where she stood she could glimpse a few boats moored in Eagle Harbor and moved over to get a better look. It was then that she looked down and saw a mailbox with the word "Semp" on it. She had seen the name before, written in a confident, feminine hand. She ran back to the car and went to the "S" section of the address book. And there it was, Semp, Ed and Jenny.

Next to the Semp mailbox were several boxes perched haphazardly on an old wooden beam. Beside the mailboxes was a dirt lane that led down to the water. Peggy left her car on the road and walked down the lane. There were four or five small houses built close to the water, looking rather old and worn from years of exposure to wind and rain and salty air. It reminded Peggy of an old-fashioned seaside village.

She found the Semp house and knocked on the door. There was no answer. She waited and knocked again and then walked around the house toward the water. She saw a gravel boat launch and a small dock. While walking down to investigate, she passed a small building. Then she remembered Deidre's words, that Mr. Ed had a "boathouse or something."

Peggy paused in front of it. The door was not locked; it was red and worn. She pulled open the door and peered into the gloom. She gasped, and her heart raced with excitement. It was Raoul's motorcycle.

"Hello," a male voice said.

For the second time that day Peggy nearly jumped out of her skin. "What? Who is it?" she blurted out.

"I think I should be askin' the questions," said a stooped man with white hair.

"I'm sorry." Peggy took several deep breaths. "I'm looking for Mr. Semp."

"He don't live in the shed."

"I know. It's just that I recognized my friend's motorcycle in there."

"I told Ed he should put a lock on that thing. That shiny motorbike would look mighty temptin' to a person who might be snoopin' around."

"Look. I know I'm probably trespassing. But it's very important that I find the man who owns that motorcycle. I understand he's a friend of Mr. Semp's."

"I wouldn't know. But I saw a guy put that motorbike in there and go off in Ed's boat."

"When?"

"Hmm. Couple days, I guess."

"Do you know when Mr. Semp is coming back?"

The man shook his head. "Couldn't say."

It didn't really matter, Peggy realized. There was only one boat and it was already gone. Peggy had to find another way to Blake Island.

As she walked back to her car she tried to think of who had a boat. It seemed to her that she had been on someone's boat only a few months ago. Of course, she thought to herself. Luke! Fourth of July. She and Raoul had gone out with Luke and Florence on Luke's boat to watch fireworks over Elliott Bay. It seemed like ages ago.

When she got to the car she fished in her purse for the business card Luke had once given her. She dialed his number and while she listened to the ring it occurred to her that Luke would mention it to Florence and Paula. No doubt the whole gang would join in the hunt for Raoul. Poor Raoul. So much for solitude.

"Excuse me, Peggy, I don't think I heard you correctly," said Luke over the phone. "It sounded like you wanted me to give you a ride to Blake Island in the boat."

"Yes. Can you do it?"

Like an astute salesman, his voice changed from confusion to warmth. "Sure, Peggy, perhaps some weekend we can organize a little outing. Were you thinking of just the two of us?"

Peggy had to remind herself that she was dealing with an extremely handsome young man who was accustomed to fending off advances from women of all ages.

"Luke, I would like to go today," said Peggy.

"Today! Wow. Let's see, I get off around five, I'll be on the five-thirty ferry..."

"Luke. I need to go now, if at all possible. You see, Raoul is camping on Blake Island and he may be in trouble. I'm asking you to give me a lift in your boat so I can check on him."

Peggy heard the distinct sound of something being deflated very quickly.

"Oh. Raoul's there?"

It amused her to think that Luke actually thought of the proposed expedition in romantic terms, a tryst on Blake Island, eating salmon by firelight with the local tribe at Tillicum Village. She had to admit she was somewhat flattered.

"I know this is very sudden, Luke," Peggy said. "But I'm worried about him and I don't know anyone else here with a boat. I suppose I could call someone in my old neighborhood in Ballard and they could motor across and pick me up. But I haven't done a very good job of keeping up with them and it would be awkward to call and say, 'Hey, can you come pick me up on Bainbridge and take me to Blake Island in your boat?'"

"Peggy, I understand. I'm looking at my calendar. I suppose I could take off, like, right now. Which would put me on the ferry in, oh, fifteen minutes. Then I need to go home and change and I could meet you at the marina after that."

"Same dock as last time? Do you remember the Fourth of July outing?"

"Yes. Same place."

"Luke, thank you so much," she said as sweetly as she could. "Tell you what, I'll bring a snack."

She could feel him blushing on the other end of the line. "Sure, happy to do it," he stammered.

Peggy sat in the driver's seat of her car. It was now a matter of waiting. She closed her eyes and allowed her breathing to settle down. She knew her stress meter was in the red territory and it worried her. Something's going on here that I don't understand, she thought. I'm overreacting to this. Why?

She started her car and drove home. When she got into her house, she put a flame under the kettle to make a fresh Thermos of tea to take on the boat. Then she checked messages; nothing new. She noticed with alarm the late hour, almost noon, and placed a container of leftover lentil soup in the microwave. She went to her bedroom and changed out of her office clothes into something more appropriate for boating and walking. It seemed absurd to be preparing for a picnic. It was even more absurd, she realized, to be choosy about what to wear, and caring for even an instant how she should look when paired with Luke, speeding across Puget Sound in his fancy Bayliner. As a matter of fact she had always believed her skin tone was just the right hue and texture for the outdoorsy, adventuresome look.

She ate her lentil soup while leaning over the kitchen sink and left the house on foot with her backpack containing tea, sunscreen, sunglasses and a hat. She stopped at Blackbird Bakery and purchased a half dozen currant tea scones. She was glad they still had them. They were her favorite alternative when she didn't have time to bake. She had a vision of greeting Raoul with scones and tea, which probably made no sense, but she didn't want to analyze her actions at that moment.

The air was cooler by the water. When she reached the dock she found a seat on a warm bench to wait for Luke. It was peaceful. The water was very still, and the few sounds of live-aboard residents going about their chores reached her ears. She looked at her watch repeatedly. What's taking Luke so long? she wondered.

She was just on the verge of dialing his number when she heard voices, in particular a certain female, nasally voice that she recognized right away.

"There you are," said Florence cheerfully.

Her outfit was so white that Peggy had to shield her eyes. Florence glowed like a snowman on a bright winter's day. One would have thought she was dressed for a yachting tour with a Greek tycoon instead of a spin across Puget Sound on Luke's motorboat.

"Hello, Florence," said Peggy, determined to be gracious.

Behind Florence was Paula in a pair of snug-fitting jeans that seemed to cover only half of her perfectly-formed rear end, and then Luke, the skipper, who was so fixated with Paula's perfectly-formed rear end that he bumped into her when she stopped. And then trailed Kelly, of all people.

"Kelly? I expected Florence and Paula. But how did you get roped into this?"

"It's Friday, and I was coming home early on the ferry and these guys kidnapped me," said Kelly.

"We're sorry for intruding, Peggy," said Paula. "We were all worried about you, especially after I told Luke about leaving you at the ferry terminal this morning."

"Gosh, that was so long ago," said Peggy.

"If you want to do this alone, we understand," said Kelly.

"I'm sure she needs moral support," said Florence. "Isn't that right, dear?"

"Yes, I'm grateful to all of you," said Peggy, feeling warm and gushy inside. "In fact, I brought scones in case anyone needs a snack."

"Perfect. I'm starved," said Kelly.

"Let's get underway," said Luke, very skipper-like.

They clambered aboard clumsily, since most of them were not experienced boaters. Luke handed around life jackets, which everyone dutifully strapped on. Once they were settled, and the boat had stopped rocking erratically, Luke eased away from the dock and motored slowly out of Eagle Harbor. Across from Luke sat Florence, exuding an air of authority appropriate to the role of the skipper's lady friend. Peggy, Paula and Kelly sat together on bench seats at the rear. Peggy gave them scones and then poured tea.

"I didn't bring extra cups so we'll have to share," said Peggy.

The group was giddy with excitement, which helped lift Peggy out of her gloom, and she began to feel grateful for their company. Then as Luke passed the mouth of the harbor and turned south and opened up the throttle, an audible cry of glee escaped involuntarily from every mouth.

Peggy held on to her hat and adjusted her sunglasses. Puget Sound shone brilliantly beneath a high midday sun. Paula zipped her jacket higher and scooted closer to Peggy.

"How did you figure out he was at Blake Island?" asked Paula, tilting her head to be heard over the wind.

"It was his daughter's suggestion. Raoul and his wife used to go camping there. I think he wanted to share a memory with her."

"When did she die?" asked Paula.

"About seven years ago."

"Isn't that a long time to, you know, still be getting over it?"

"You never get over it," said Peggy. "When you find the perfect mate in life, someone you are truly in love with, and then you lose that person, the feeling you have is that he or she was your one love and there will never be another."

"That's so romantic," said Paula. "Everlasting love. So what do you do about it? How do you get on with your life?"

Peggy smiled. She had been asking the same question for a year. "That's the funny thing about the grieving process. It's not always a case of sitting around wiping away tears and being sad. There's a definite period for that, of course, but what really happens over a longer period is that you feel unsettled, like your life isn't back to normal. You make bad decisions, bad choices. Your judgment is lousy. You feel disoriented. You have trouble making new friends. You're a mess, quite frankly."

"So, do you think he's still going through that?" asked Paula.

"I think we both are, and that's why we have trouble keeping up this relationship. We would each prefer to have our lost loves back."

"That's awful," said Paula.

"I think it can be even worse with men. They sometimes don't get to the acceptance phase. They get stuck in the middle phase because they don't recognize it as part of grief. They become disoriented without knowing why, or what to do about it."

Paula lowered her voice and leaned even closer to Peggy's ear. "That makes sense because I think men are basically fragile creatures when you get right down to it."

Peggy laughed. "You are very wise for a young woman."

Luke looked back from the wheel. "There's Blake. It won't be long now."

Peggy gazed ahead toward the island. She wondered what Raoul was doing. She imagined him sitting beside his little pup tent, reading a book or cooking fish, enjoying an escape from society. But most of all, she worried about his reaction upon having them descend upon him. Would he be angry?

As the boat neared Blake Island, Peggy moved forward, unsteadily, and gripped the back of Luke's seat with one hand while holding on to her hat with the other. The island seemed desolate, prehistoric, a place where ancient rituals might be performed in great secrecy. She felt like a trespasser, and it filled her with dread. What am I doing here? she wondered.

They spotted another boat coming toward them from the island. It was just a blurry dot at first, possibly a buoy. But the shape gradually became larger and more identifiable: a small motorboat. Luke altered course to the right to give it room, and slowed his speed so as not to generate too large a wake. The oncoming boat swerved to starboard as well.

The two boats closed the gap rapidly. Peggy stood behind Luke, on the right side of their boat, shading her eyes to get a better view. She saw two figures in the other boat. It bounced lightly on the surface of the water.

Finally it was almost abreast of them, then almost past them, when Peggy recognized a familiar outline, a face with a beard, a familiar jacket.

Peggy shouted. "That's Raoul!" She waved. "Raoul!" she yelled. She saw his head turn, the upper part of his face obscured by sunglasses and a hat. She did not recognize the other man with him.

Florence stood up quickly, too quickly, just as Luke executed a U-turn sharply to the left. Florence let out a scream as she fell back.

Peggy turned. Florence reached wildly for something to grab. Anything. Peggy saw that she was going over. Luke was preoccupied with steering the boat.

Florence hit the rail with her backside and began to tumble. Her left hand swung into the air. Peggy reached for it but missed. With a shriek of terror, Florence disappeared over the side of the boat. Peggy heard a splash.

"Luke, she went over!" Peggy yelled.

Kelly ran forward and leaned over the rail but was too late to reach her; the boat had too much speed. Luke yanked the throttle and turned the wheel hard to circle back. Florence bobbed in the water like a cork with a wet mop of hair. Peggy saw that Florence's life vest was keeping her afloat.

Meanwhile, the boat containing Raoul had steered toward them and reached Florence before Luke could finish executing his turn. With two burly arms hooked under hers, Raoul fished a dripping Florence out of the water. Luke pulled closer and killed his engine. Peggy could see Florence's pale face speckled with goose bumps. She shivered. Pieces of kelp clung to her white outfit. Her breath came in gasps.

The man with Raoul, who Peggy presumed was Ed Semp, had already unzipped a large sleeping bag and spread it on a bench. Raoul set Florence into it and tucked her legs inside and then zipped her up so that only her head poked out of it, with her latest hairdo now plastered flat against her temples.

"Florence, are you okay?" Peggy called out to her.

Florence nodded, then started breathing normally. "I think I'll survive." She smiled gratefully at Raoul. "Thanks to my rescuer."

Raoul shrugged. "We happened to get to you first."

His sunglasses now removed, Raoul's expression was a mixture of bewilderment and concern, but with a trace of amusement. They all stood staring at each other for a very long moment. Peggy began to have the sinking feeling that she had made a huge mistake. Raoul didn't look very lost. Being rescued appeared to be the furthest thing from his mind.

"Well, hello, Raoul. Fancy meeting you in the middle of Puget Sound on a Friday afternoon," said Peggy with a weak smile.

Raoul motioned to his companion. "This is Ed Semp, a very dear friend for many years. Ed, these are my commuting friends from the ferry." He introduced them all, starting with Florence and going around until he got to Peggy. "...and this is Peggy."

Ed's eyes rested on her and he said, "Ah."

Peggy wanted to hide under a seat cushion.

Florence coughed.

Ed said, "We need to get this young lady to shore. Do you have a car at the dock, Miss?"

A bit of color rushed into Florence's face. "I can't remember the last time somebody called me 'Miss.' Yes, I do."

"I'm dying to know how you all happen to be out for a pleasure cruise in Luke's boat on a Friday afternoon," said Raoul. "But I'm afraid the story will have to wait." He turned to Ed. "Ready?"

"Nice meetin' you folks," said Ed Semp with a wave. Ed started his boat.

Peggy handed over Florence's purse. As Raoul took it from her he said, "Can I call you later? I want to tell you about my week."

"I'd like to hear about it," she said. She wasn't sure of her feelings at that moment. She was relieved that he wasn't lost or injured, or on a rendezvous with another woman, but at the same time she felt a little annoyed at his being absent without telling anyone, even his daughter. Peggy couldn't help noticing that Florence seemed actually thrilled to have been rescued by Raoul. It struck Peggy once again that Florence was, in many ways, the perfect midlife partner for Raoul.

Peggy was not very talkative as they returned to the dock in Luke's boat and disembarked. She thanked everyone for coming along and said over and over how much she appreciated their company. They all hugged her and wished her well. Then she returned home on foot, walking quickly and purposefully.

She entered her house knowing her next move. She called her boss.

"Milton?" she said.

"Peggy. Yes, yes. How are you? Did you find Raoul?"

"Yes. We got all that straightened out. The reason I'm calling is about the dinner. Is it still on?"

"You bet. I have reservations for two at Wild Ginger," said Milton excitedly.

"Can you add one more?"

"You?"

"Yes, I would like to go, if it's okay."

Milton's voice was filled with relief. "You don't know how happy I am to hear that."

"I gave it some thought and decided I'm not quite ready to burn my bridges, as they say."

"Well in that case, let me tell you something I didn't mention before. By the way, wear something nice tonight because this is really an interview."

"What kind of interview?" said Peggy.

"Dr. Hinckley has offered us a one-year residency at his research center in Woods Hole."

Peggy gasped. She knew it was a once-in-a-lifetime opportunity. The charming seaside town of Woods Hole was the Center of the Universe as far as many climate-change researchers were concerned.

"Yes. You heard me correctly."

"A year in Woods Hole! That's amazing. But I'm not a scientist," she said.

"That's okay. This residency is focused on using data to propose and debate policy. You're a genius at that."

"Don't get carried away, Milton."

"Look, I haven't formally nominated you. But I want to see what kind of rapport you can establish with Dr. Hinckley. If you guys hit it off, and you want to go, you let me know in private. Deal?"

"Okay. Deal. But I'm not making any promises."

"Thanks, Peg. See you at the restaurant at seven o'clock."

Peggy hung up and took a shower. She stood under the warm water for a long time to wash off the salty sea air from Puget Sound. Then, dressed in her robe, she opened her closet.

There was really only one option: black, with some kind of flattering color on top. She chose a black skirt and black heels and a soft blouse the color of emerald-green water. I'll look like I belong in Woods Hole, she thought. She rummaged and found a clasp for her hair that matched her shoes, and a sparkling pendant that would look smart over the blouse. She laid everything on her bed and studied it critically. She pulled on the skirt and checked herself in the mirror. Too short? Or too long?

The phone rang. It was Raoul. She sat on her bed.

"Can I fix dinner for you tonight?" he asked.

"I have a business dinner to attend, at Wild Ginger."

"Nice. Must be an important guest."

"Yes. Milton's all worked up about it. I can't say no."

Pause. "I have some important things to say, and I wanted to say them in person."

"Have you called Deidre?" Peggy asked.

"Yes. I got an earful."

"Are you surprised?"

"I suppose I should have left word."

"That would have been helpful."

"You're sore at me, aren't you?"

"That's putting it mildly. I've just spent the most frustrating day of my life and it's not even over yet."

"Can I see you?"

"I'm busy getting ready for my dinner. I have to rest and collect my thoughts."

"Okay, then, I'll say what I have to say."

She waited. He cleared his throat.

"You see, I was having dinner with Ed Semp earlier this week and he made an observation. He told me that I had never gotten over Priscilla's death. I told him he was crazy. Of course I had gotten over it. Then Ed proposed that we go camping and talk about it. So we did. We kind of just got up and went without much planning. Once we were out there, Ed told me all the reasons why he thought that was true. It was mostly things I've said over the years to him, and things I've done. He's known me long enough, before and after Priscilla, to recognize I wasn't being honest with myself. After a couple of days, I began to believe he was right."

Raoul continued, breathlessly. Peggy realized he had been saving this up and she let him have his say. "Bottom line, Peggy, is that I feel much better about things, but I don't think it would have happened without you. You got me out of my shell over these past few months. Especially when you brought up the idea of that club of yours. I was very negative about it, but later I realized the problem was me: I was too wrapped up in my own world, still living with Priscilla. I didn't want any intruders. You have helped me more than you know. You have turned my life around."

Her mood softened.

"I've been a jerk for years, and along comes one person, you, and it's reversed."

"People don't turn their lives around on a dime," she said. "It may be the beginning of a reversal, perhaps, but I wouldn't assume you're done."

"But I can see where it's going, and I can see what an impact you've had." He paused again. She sensed something big was coming. "I wonder if we could discuss a new arrangement between us."

"Like?"

"Would you like to move in with me?" The words came out rushed, and she felt bad that he had to say them over the phone.

"I suppose it would be a bit like having your own personal trainer right in your house," she said.

"Peggy, I knew this would be misunderstood..."

"No, I understand perfectly. Whenever you get depressed I cheer you up. Is that it? Well, who's going to cheer me up? I don't see anyone helping me with my issues. Believe me, I've learned today that I still have issues."

"I want to help you. We need to help each other."

"That's not the basis for a relationship; it sounds more like a dependency. I don't want to be on drugs. I want to be healthy."

"Are you sure you don't have just ten minutes to meet with me?"

"And besides, where would this lead? Is this one of these sex-with-no-commitment deals?"

"I didn't think you'd be interested in marriage."

Peggy thought for a moment. "I can't answer that. In fact, if you had proposed marriage I would be dropping the phone and running for my life. To be honest, I prefer the idea of living with you. But it has to feel right. It has to feel healthy and loving, and not like two clueless people depending on each other for emotional sanity."

They were silent for several long seconds. Peggy played with the hem of her skirt and tested how it looked when she crossed her legs. It does ride up fairly high, she observed.

"There's not much else I have to say," he said at last.

"I'm sorry for being cross with you. I need to take a nap and go to my dinner. And I'll call you this weekend."

"Deal," he said.

Peggy observed that it was the second deal she was offered that day. It was a day of deals. What else was in store for her?

She slipped out of her skirt and crawled into bed after setting the alarm clock. She woke up an hour later, feeling somewhat refreshed, and carefully applied a small amount of makeup and lipstick, thinking, Hmm, Wild Ginger is rather dark, and then dressed for her outing. She drank a cup of tea slowly, replaying in her mind the key points of the ocean temperature research, the "cocktail conversation," as Milton would call it.

When it was time to go she put extra cash in her purse for the taxi ride from the ferry terminal to the restaurant. She slipped a dark cashmere coat around her shoulders and checked herself once more in the mirror. She was beautiful.

****

It was close to midnight when Peggy stood on the sidewalk in front of a small First Avenue bar and shook hands with Dr. Hanford Hinckley. Milton jabbered excitedly at her elbow.

"It certainly was our pleasure, Dr. Hinckley," Milton was saying.

Peggy hardly heard him. Instead, she was struck, as she had been all evening, by how Dr. Hinckley reminded her of Taylor.

For one thing, Dr. Hinckley was totally preoccupied. Even now he looked at his watch as though he had a midnight appointment to keep. Taylor had had the same kind of manner: alert and probing, yet his brain, like a computer, could run a background process while he talked about, say, his favorite oysters. In fact, that was one of the topics Dr. Hinckley expounded on for twenty minutes while they sipped martinis. The similarities gave Peggy the creeps; she was glad Milton was there.

"I hope to see you in January," he said.

Peggy smiled. "I'm giving it serious thought. It's very exciting, Dr. Hinckley."

"I think you'd do well," he said.

They parted, and Milton drove Peggy to the ferry. She felt herself falling asleep as soon as she sat in Milton's car.

"What'd ya think?" said Milton.

"Brilliant. Intimidating. He's too bright to have an ordinary conversation with. Have you ever heard someone toss off so many facts and figures about ocean warming?"

"No. I haven't."

"I felt like a graduate student going to dinner with her professor."

"If you want my opinion..."

"I know your opinion, Milt. You want me to take it."

"It would be great for the organization, and great for you."

"Oh? Why would it be great for me?"

"You need a break from here. Too many memories."

"Some of the memories are good."

"But some of them aren't."

Peggy fell silent. She knew he was telling the truth. There had been times, since Taylor's death, when Peggy was feeling blue, and Milton had been the one to remind her of the things she didn't like about her marriage, the things she had complained about at the office. Peggy's standard response to Milton was always, "no relationship is perfect."

"No relationship is perfect," she told him.

"Exactly my point. Why do it again?"

"What do you mean?"

"I'm talking about Raoul. I didn't realize how serious it was until today. All I'm saying is, before you jump into another relationship, be sure you know what you are doing. That's why I think living somewhere else for a while would not be a bad idea."

Peggy was stunned. Why was it that other people always saw her situation more clearly than she saw it herself?

FIFTEEN

Saturday, October 15

PEGGY SLEPT MUCH LATER THAN usual. As she lay in bed with her eyes open she was struck, once again, by the good fortune that had come her way. Now all that remained was to decide whether to spend a year in Massachusetts. She would be closer to Marjorie and Taylor, Jr., and there had been persistent rumors that Marjorie and Stan were trying to start a family. She certainly wanted to be on hand to provide motherly advice, asked for or not.

She got out of bed and made tea. The phone beckoned. She knew she had to face Raoul. She looked out of the window at a grayish day. Then she lifted the receiver and dialed.

"Hello?" His voice sounded cheerful.

"Good morning," she said.

"How was Wild Ginger?" His voice was pleasant, too pleasant, like a salesman's.

"Delicious, as usual. Our visiting scientist was very interesting and important, so Milton pulled out all the stops. There's lots to tell; a lot has happened."

"Well, I'd like to hear about it."

"I'm not so sure. I've been offered a one-year residency in Massachusetts, at a research institute."

A long silence. Then, "I guess that means you're not moving in?"

Peggy found herself wishing he had said something different, something more congratulatory. She wanted him to be proud of her, not thinking of how her news affected him.

"I haven't decided," she replied. "But I really called to say something else. There's a certain conversation we said we would have. We discussed it in New Orleans. Remember?"

"Priscilla and Taylor," he said.

"Yes."

One hour later they stood looking down the shoreline at Fay Bainbridge, where, just a day earlier, Peggy had conducted her futile search for Raoul. It was not as windy, just gray and calm.

"What I will never, ever forget," she began, "was the suddenness of Taylor's death. We were having a conversation, it was about Marjorie, and choosing a date to visit her in Virginia. I was about to call Marjorie to see what was okay. It was in my mind to do that. I still remember stopping to think about what time it was in Virginia; I didn't want to call too late because she goes to bed early. And I said to him 'Okay, the 5th it is,' and he didn't answer. I thought at first he had changed his mind about the date. I looked at him and his eyes started to close, like he was very sleepy. I went to him, thinking I should make him take a nap. That's when he fainted. His head started to fall forward. I caught him. Never did it cross my mind that that was the last conversation I would have with him. I called 9-1-1 and rode with him to the hospital. He never regained consciousness. I refused to believe he was gone. My brain and my heart couldn't accept it. I lived in denial for months. I couldn't let go. I suppose the hardest part of all was that we didn't say good-bye."

She drank water from a plastic bottle and pulled a crumpled tissue out of her pocket. The tears seemed to blend with the salty air.

"Thanks for listening," she said.

He said. "My experience was almost exactly the opposite. Priscilla died a long slow death from breast cancer. It happened over a one-year period. First came the diagnosis. I was in immediate denial from the start, thinking it was an illness that would pass. Then the treatments and long stays in the hospital, which grew longer as she grew weaker. She went from being the most vibrant, active woman anybody knew to simply a human shell with all the life drained out of it. After a point she wanted no visitors except family. It was too shocking. Myself and Deidre and Priscilla's sister were with her when she took her last breath." He paused. "You said that you didn't say good-bye to Taylor; I said good-bye for a year. I'm not sure which is worse. It was especially hard on Deidre. God, it was awful to see her with her mother. I would have given anything in the world to reverse what was happening, just for Deidre's sake. Frankly, she's not over it. I still worry about her."

They sat on a large piece of driftwood and watched a bit of pale sunlight peek from behind a cloud.

"What about you? Are you over it?" asked Peggy at last. Pause. "No. I'm not."

She smiled. "You know, I thought I was so superior and now I feel so foolish."

"Why?"

"Because I thought I had accepted Taylor's death and you were the one still in denial. I thought I was helping you, when in fact I was the one who needed help. I thought I was in control, but I haven't been."

"What makes you say that?"

"It's the way I've been behaving, reaching for something, grasping at straws. I think I was using you to avoid looking at myself. You became a welcome distraction. Instead of dwelling on my own loss, and getting healthy, I could pretend to be helping you with yours, instead. Does that make sense?"

Raoul thought about Peggy's words. "I see. I was a smoke screen."

"But the screen disappeared this week. I saw myself clearly for the first time in a long time."

They sat silently together; Peggy wasn't keeping track of the passing of time. She felt a burden lift itself magically from her mind and body and she wanted to enjoy the fleeting moment of lightness.

She took a deep breath. "I suppose I should tell you about the residency in Massachusetts."

She explained the proposition and described her meeting with Dr. Hinckley. Of course, she knew what Raoul's question would be: "What do you want to do?" She didn't yet have an answer.

Thursday, November 24, Thanksgiving Day

With a festive *Pop!*, Raoul ejected the cork from the sparkling wine and sent it flying out the back door.

Florence almost choked on a piece of salmon and goat cheese. "My God, are you shooting the turkey?"

Raoul poured bubbly golden liquid into Champagne flutes and passed them around. He wore a blue blazer with gold buttons and a neatly pressed shirt. "This is an impressive brut from Italy."

Florence took the glass. "I've always wanted to spend Thanksgiving with an Italian brute."

"I'll drink to that," said Paula.

"As long as he's a well-mannered brute," said Peggy, raising her glass to touch Paula's.

Xena came from the kitchen bearing a plate of fresh pears and sharp cheese. "Wait a minute, I want to be in on any discussion of brutes, well-mannered or otherwise."

The women laughed as their glasses touched.

Raoul looked at Kelly and Luke. "Should we go for a walk or something?"

"We'd have to slouch," said Kelly, "in order to look more brutish."

Luke said, "Next time, just get white wine."

Raoul cleared his throat. "Are you ladies quite done?"

"We haven't even started," said Florence, winking at Raoul.

"I believe a toast to Peggy is in order," said Raoul.

"To Peggy in her new home," said Paula.

They raised their glasses toward Peggy.

"You got guts, honey," said Florence.

"Bravo," said Xena.

Raoul put his glass down. "I'd better check the turkey."

"I'll come with you," said Kelly.

Peggy watched them go outside to the grill and lift the lid. The aroma of roasting turkey wafted through the open door, along with a gust of cold air. She closed the door and looked through the glass. The rain had not yet started but she could feel it coming. The landscape was gray and misty, with subdued patches of color.

The morning had been a rush. She made her favorite apple and sage dressing while Raoul got the turkey ready and then started a complicated stock for the gravy. Paula came early and made mashed potatoes. Xena brought appetizers. Florence picked up wine from the store, after receiving detailed instructions from Raoul.

Peggy walked away from the window toward the hallway, where a row of suitcases was lined up. Waiting. Paula came over.

"It's hard to tell if you're coming or going," said Paula.

Peggy laughed. "I'm in transit. I had to clear out of my house yesterday so the new tenant could move in."

"You mean, you're actually giving up the house?" asked Paula.

"Except for the luggage you see here, all my worldly possessions are either in storage or en route to Massachusetts."

Paula looked at her with admiration. "I'm so proud of you." But then Paula tilted her head in the direction of Raoul, who was still outside.

Peggy understood the question. "He's being a good sport, very supportive, actually, once he figured out that my mind was made up."

Raoul and Kelly came through the door on a gust of cold air and roasting turkey.

"Make way for the turkey," said Kelly.

"Which one?" said Florence.

Xena laughed. "Raoul, your guests are so entertaining."

"Depends on which end of the jokes you're on," he said.

"Should I start the vegetables?" said Paula.

"I'll open the wine," said Florence.

"But save some for the rest of us," said Raoul.

Xena laughed again. "You two belong in a sitcom."

"What can I do?" asked Peggy. "My dressing is hot; I'll just turn the oven off."

"Stir the gravy, if you have a moment," said Raoul.

Florence gazed into the refrigerator. "These desserts look deadly. What are they?"

"Pumpkin crème brûlée," said Raoul.

"Are they creamy and fatty and loaded with calories?" asked Florence.

"You bet, especially after I glaze them using my new kitchen torch."

"Good. I'm splurging this weekend."

"Monday's a long way off," said Xena. "You can get back into your girdle by then."

"Um, that implies exercise," said Florence.

For about twenty minutes, they wore a path between the kitchen and the dining room, setting out the Thanksgiving feast on a pressed, pale yellow tablecloth laden with crystal wine glasses and monogrammed silver and plates rimmed in white gold.

"Your wedding china?" asked Florence of Raoul.

"Yes. Priscilla picked it out. I really should give it to Deidre."

"It's beautiful."

In the center of the table, a great vase of alstroemeria caught the gray light from the windows and sprayed the ivory-colored plates with dots of Fall color. Peggy moved the vase to a side table near the window.

"Wonderful flowers, Peggy," said Xena.

Peggy was preoccupied as she forced her attention back to the dining table. "I feel like I'm forgetting something."

Once the dishes of food were arranged on the crowded table like pieces of a puzzle, Raoul invited everyone to sit. They enjoyed a round of toasting and shared thoughts of thankfulness. Then they noisily handed around platters and bowls of turkey, gravy, fresh cranberry sauce, crisp green beans, and mashed potatoes. Peggy couldn't shake the thought that something was missing.

"Ah, the new wine of the vintage," Raoul said, raising a glass of 2005 Beaujolais Nouveau. "Look at the rich purple color, and the nose is very fruity. It's a great year for grapes, in France at least."

"To tell you the truth," said Florence, "I haven't met a year I didn't like."

"Hence, my detailed instructions regarding the wine," said Raoul.

"Really, dear, I think you would graciously consume any wine that I brought over because you're such a gentleman," said Florence. "And after the third glass, you would think I was an absolute wine connoisseur." Florence took very small bites of food as she talked.

Peggy sipped the wine. "It is good. I just wish I could remember what it is we're missing."

Kelly said, "You're distracted. We understand."

"Are you going straight to Massachusetts?" asked Luke.

"I'm detouring in Virginia, first, to spend December with my daughter and her husband. Then I'll spend a few days in Brooklyn with my son, and then go to Woods Hole after the first of the year."

"Just in time for blizzards," said Xena, shivering.

"A good excuse to update your wardrobe," said Florence.

"Exactly," said Peggy.

Florence then turned serious. "Peggy, do you mind sharing how you made this decision to go wandering off to godforsaken places?"

Peggy laughed, then composed her thoughts. The room was suddenly quiet. "The last few months have been the most... therapeutic, I guess, that I've spent in the last year-and-a-half. I came to realize that I was in denial over my husband's death. It started to hit me when we were in New Orleans with Raoul's sister, grieving for her friend, Agnes Lambert. I imagined how when a person dies, their soul leaves the body and goes on living in a different place, and it's easy to feel as though you are still with that person in spirit, especially if it's someone you were deeply in love with. I realized, later, that I was still living with Taylor in that way. I shared my thoughts with him, I had conversations with him. The problem is that I began to realize that the rest of my life, my physical life here on Earth, had just stopped. Although I still love Taylor dearly, I don't want the rest of my life to grind to a halt while I wait to join him in spirit."

She paused for a breath and sipped water. Paula dabbed her eyes with a napkin. Peggy continued. "So, the point is, and I hope you don't think I'm being selfish, I'm going off to do something for myself, something rewarding and intellectually challenging, something I've always dreamed of doing. Frankly, I think Taylor would be very proud of me."

"And we are very proud of you as well," said Raoul. All eyes turned to him. Waiting.

Raoul got up from the table. "I have something to give each of you." Peggy wondered what he was up to as he withdrew what looked like a stack of postcards from the pocket of his corduroy sport coat.

"This is an invitation to join a new and exciting organization," he began. As he walked around the table he handed one to Kelly, whose eyes lit up.

He handed one to Xena and she said, "How beautiful."

Peggy could not see what they were looking at.

"It's an organization with a bold mission statement, an ambitious plan to get people to think about how they live and how they use precious natural resources."

He handed a card to Florence and she said, "Wait, I've seen that."

Peggy was now consumed with curiosity. She leaned over to see what Florence was holding.

Raoul handed one to Luke, then Paula, and then paused by Peggy's chair with a single card remaining in his hand.

"Peggy, this new organization needs a leader with a vision, and I can think of no one better suited than you. Especially since it was your idea to begin with."

"What are you talking about?" She snatched the card from his hands, and her mouth froze in mid-sentence. Across the top was a colorful montage of photographs, many of them taken by Raoul over the months since they had met. She recognized a picture of her own hands picking blackberries. There was a shot of the shrimp stew they had made, the purple clematis from Raoul's garden, a girl dancing in Maine in front of the Crannies' house, a produce stand at the Pike Place Market, and, rising above all of that, a brilliant orange and yellow morning sky with the city of Seattle in the foreground: It was her favorite morning view from the ferry. Tears streamed down her cheeks. She wiped them with a tissue. Beneath the montage, a few lines of text were engraved in gold letters:

Announcing the formation of SEA CHANGES, a society devoted to changing the way people think about how they live.

Beneath the text was a smaller montage containing pictures from the Tabard Inn and a menu from the Camellia Grill in New Orleans. In the background was a picture of the Manhattan Bridge that Raoul had taken on his morning walk across the Brooklyn Bridge. Here, in one small space, was a representation of their most important experiences together.

Peggy stood and hugged Raoul. She didn't bother to wipe the tears, there were too many of them. The dining room chairs rattled as everyone stood and applauded.

When the applause died down, Peggy said, "What does this mean? Are you starting a Zkclub?"

"No, I would like to help you start your club," he said. "I think you had a great idea, and I'd like to help you work on it. That is, if you'll still have me as a member."

Florence said, "I think that means he wants to visit."

Peggy said to Raoul, "Of course I still want you as a member. And all of you are welcome, for short visits."

Raoul held up his hands. "I'm not hinting at any such thing. I believe you should have your time to do something you've always wanted to do. As for me, I'm thinking of going to New Mexico to rent a cabin in the desert and paint pictures. I, too, need to roam a bit and do something I've always wanted to do."

Florence brightened. "That sounds lovely. Do you need an assistant?"

"No."

Everyone laughed. Peggy raised her glass. "Now it's my turn to propose a toast, to all of you, for being such wonderful friends. I love you all, and I will miss you."

Their glasses touched with bright tones that resonated throughout the room. Then Peggy almost choked on her wine as a thought hit her. "My dressing! We forgot the dressing!"

She rushed to the oven and opened it. Although the oven had been turned off, the pungent odor told her that the food had sat in the still-hot oven too long. With two pot holders, she lifted out the long dish and carried it into the dining room. They all stared at a brown, well-cooked mixture with a dark, syrupy sludge at the bottom of the pan.

"Smells approximately like apples," said Xena.

"It is, or was, my apple-sage-caramelized-onion dressing."

Peggy looked up with a smile. "You know what? I'm so happy at this moment I don't even care."